I0533957

Montana Skirts

Books Published by Chance Cooper:

McCart Series:
Logan's Vengeance (1st Book in Series)
Cottonwood Pass (2nd Book in Series)

Other Books:
Montana Skirts

Montana Skirts

Alejandra was raised under the harsh conditions of the Chihuahua Desert in Mexico. Her mother died at birth and she was raised by her father, who taught her how to ride, rope and shoot as well as any man. Her father has since been murdered, and she is no longer capable of maintaining the herd on the parched desert land. She has decided to drive the herd 1500 miles north to the Montana Territory to start a new life.

Along the way she encounters rapists, kidnappers, a child slaver and Indians. And amidst all that, she builds a formidable ranch and finds her true love.

But first, she must save his life, and then he must save her.

Montana Skirts

Written By
Chance Cooper

Published by: Books By Chance

ISBN-10: 0-9963931-0-2

ISBN-13: 978-0-9963931-0-2

Montana Skirts

Dedicated to my loving wife:

Catherine

Chapter 1

It's a cool sunny day, late in the spring of 1857. Corey Kittridge lies face down in the high Montana grass, bleeding to death from the arrows sticking out his back. His string of Spanish Andalusian horses, the big grey stallion he was riding and three solid black mares, were taken by the Sioux Indians that attacked him.

Corey was riding easy in the saddle, enjoying the scenery while considering the land as a prime location to build his horse ranch. Day dreaming, he was unaware of the Sioux war party approaching him from the other side of the hill. They appeared suddenly as Corey topped the hill. He knew instantly his chances of survival were slim as he made a quick count of five braves. He could release the mares to free himself up to fight and possibly defeat the warriors, or he could try and outrun them with the mares in tow. He chose to run, even though Corey is an excellent shot, he knows how difficult it is to shoot from a moving horse. Sure he would kill two, maybe three of them, but the numbers were in their favor and they were skilled warriors who didn't fear death. So even taking a few losses, the Indians wouldn't quit until he was dead, and they had his horses.

The Sioux were as unaware of Corey's presence as he had been of theirs. They were in Crow Territory looking to steal horses from the Crow. It was widely known, especially between the Indian tribes, that the Crow were excellent horsemen and maintained great herds. Upon seeing the white man and the magnificent horses he was trailing, they charged up the hill after him.

Corey wheeled his stallion and headed back down the hill. He was looking for a spot that would provide

1

protection for himself and his horses while he mounted a defense. He could have easily out run the Sioux if he had just let go of the mares, but the horses were the only thing he had left from his dad and their ranch in Texas. They were his start to a new life. He had no intention of giving them up without a fight. The problem was, he couldn't turn in the saddle and return fire while riding at a dead run. Besides, his spare hand was holding the lead rope attached to his mares. The Sioux quickly overtook him, and with precise shooting, put three arrows in him.

Loosing strength from his wounds Corey fell out of the saddle. Unable to break his fall, he was knocked out when he hit the ground. Being unconscious he remained non-responsive to the pokes delivered to his ribs by the Indians bows. As a result, the Sioux believed Corey was dead. Otherwise they would have killed him for sure.

The Andalusian is a beautiful Spanish horse with a long flowing mane. They are an athletic breed that possess great strength and stamina. The Andalusian was bred specifically for herding the dangerous Vista Hermosa fighting bulls of Spain. Corey's horses are the offspring of the pure bred Spanish Andalusian horses his father brought over from England.

Whether you want to say it's fate, or preordained, certain events happen that bring two people together. Under normal circumstances the same people may never have met or appealed to one another. Such is the case with Alejandra Strand and Corey Kittridge.

Alejandra and Corey were both born and raised on small Texas ranches. While the ranches were located over a hundred miles apart, their families struggled against the same hardships. Bandits, Indians, overbearing land barons and ranchers, and drought. Not to mention they both lost their mother at an early age and were raised by their father.

Chapter 2

Alejandra's father, Klaus Strand, migrated to America from Germany in 1825. Bias and discrimination on the eastern seaboard forced him to change his given name from Klaus to Eli, and to change his speech dialect. He moved westward in 1827, where he tried to squeak out a living in the parched lands of the Chihuahua Desert. The area was still part of Mexico at the time and mostly populated by Mexican citizens. Although they would win their independence in 1836, and become part of the Republic of Texas.

In 1830, three years after staking his claim to a patch of desert land no one else wanted, Eli fell in love and married Catalina Alejandro, a beautiful Spanish woman with coal black hair and green eyes.

Catalina gave birth to Alejandra, a beautiful little girl on September 28, 1832. They named her after Alejandro, meaning the "Great Conqueror", to honor Catalina's surname which means "Defender of Man". The birth was extremely hard on Catalina and she never regained her health. Two years after giving birth to Alejandra, she died.

Eli gave all his attention and love to Alejandra, and never married again. Inexperienced with raising a child, especially a girl, he raised Alejandra the same as he would have raised a son. He taught her to ride, shoot, and rope and brand. She became an all around cowgirl. Aside from performing all the ranch activities, Eli taught her how to survive in the wild in case he was killed, or died from disease. Eli never considered it would be Trent Oswald, Alejandra's childhood friend, and the son of their neighbor, that would be the cause of his demise.

In the summer of 1849, the rain, although always sparse in that part of the desert, had been almost non-existent this year. The stock tanks were either low or empty, in either case, there was not enough to support even the smallest herd. Eli, along with his lone ranch hand Octavio, moved his herd to the Pecos river for water. Normally Alejandra would accompany her father to the river, but this trip he insisted she remain back at the house. He was concerned for her safety, because there had been several citing's of bandits and Indians crossing the river as of late. In times of drought, bandits and Indians frequently traveled the Pecos river as they traveled back and forth across the Rio Grand to rustle cattle and horses. However, both groups were notorious for kidnapping women to sale in Mexico when the opportunity presented itself.

The Strand's herd was made up of two hundred longhorns. A small herd, mostly because their ranch would not support a larger herd. Although, it was big enough to provide for them, and allowed them to live far away from the prejudices he experienced in the east, and larger towns in the west.

Their neighbor, Lucas Oswald, owned most of the land in the area. He had forced out most of the small ranchers by controlling the water. This included access to the Rio Grand. Yet, while he was ambitious and self serving, he had never resorted to, or advocated the use of violence. The same could not be said for his son Trent.

Alejandra and Trent grew up as childhood friends. The Chihuahua desert was especially tough on the weak and women. Trent's mother also died when he was young, although his upbringing was far different than Alejandra's. His father spoiled him, overlooking his poor attitude toward others and believing he could do nothing wrong. Without his mother's guidance, and his father turning a blind eye to his notoriously bad behavior, Trent became mean and thought himself superior to others. Doted on by his father, and with the Oswald ranch being the largest in the territory, Trent believed he was entitled to whatever he wanted and that it should be given to him without question.

Trent's mean spirited behavior was what drove Alejandra and him apart. Not having to share in most of the ranch work, Trent spent endless hours practicing his quick draw and target shooting. Up until now, his shootings had been restricted to the Oswald ranch, and the killings had been classified as justified in protecting the ranch from cattle rustlers. However, a few of the killings where questionable as to whether the men involved were really rustling cattle, or were just travelers caught up in Trent's thirst for killing. Regardless of evidence to the contrary, the killings were never challenged. Mostly because the town folk and other ranchers feared Trent would retaliate against the accusers.

Trent fancied himself a ladies man. He was a handsome young man with golden hair and blue eyes, standing just over six feet tall. His self righteous attitude turned off most of the girls, especially Alejandra. Once a valued friend, she now feels nothing but contempt for him. She was always holding her father up as an example to Trent of how a man should present himself and treat a woman. This always irritated Trent, causing him to admonish Alejandra for being an uppity dirt farmer.

Trent always had it in his mind that he would eventually marry Alejandra. If for no other reason, for the Oswald wealth that would be bestowed upon her, but also because of his egotistical nature and the limited number of available young men in Val Verde County. It never entered his mind that Alejandra had come to hate him, and wanted nothing more to do with him, let alone marry him.

Alejandra inherited her mother's beautiful smooth creamy skin and bright green eyes. She got her blonde hair and tall stature from her father. At five foot eight inches, Alejandra was an intimidating figure. Having been raised by her father, with no mother to provide a feminine side, she exhibited the same traits as him. This included a fiery temper, along with a great internal strength. After Trent killed his first man, an unarmed pioneer, she felt nothing but disgust and contempt for him.

Had the killing been in defense of himself, or to keep his herd from being rustled, she would have accepted the killing. But his ways of bullying, and shooting a defenseless pioneer under questionable circumstances, made her question his morals. It left her somewhat afraid of him at the same time.

Chapter 3

Eli left Octavio with the herd down at the river, while he rode back up the banks to set up camp for the night. He had just gotten the campfire started when he heard the horse's footfalls behind him. Eli was bent over the fire with his back to the approaching rider. Naturally he believed the rider to be Octavio, so he remained bend over stoking the fire as he addressed the rider.

"Octavio, why aren't you down at the river watching the cattle?"

When there was no response he turned around, only to be surprised to see Trent Oswald sitting his horse, starring down at him. Something within him told him he was in serious trouble.

"Howdy, Mr. Strand. Where is your daughter, doesn't she usually come to the river with you?"

"She stayed home this trip."

Eli had hoped this information would send Trent on his way, but it didn't. Trent grinned, in a way that showed his contempt for Mr. Strand, then he spoke again.

"I came out here to ask you for your daughter's hand in marriage Mr. Strand. Knowing you wouldn't want to live apart from her, I am offering to build you a house on the Oswald ranch after we are married. You will be able to live your remaining days in comfort, while at the same time remaining close to your daughter."

Eli didn't hold back his thoughts.

"You really think I can be bribed into giving Alejandra's hand away in marriage. When it comes to who she chooses to marry, that will be her decision, not mine? Besides, she detests you and wants nothing at all to do with you. She has refused your advances, so you thought by offering me a small cabin on the great Oswald Ranch, that you could convince her to change her mind. I would never give you my blessings to marry Alejandra. Just as she does, I believe you are a mean spirited individual, and it is also my belief that you would mistreat and abuse my daughter. My answer is no, and there is nothing you can offer me to change mine, or my daughters, mind."

Eli's rejection and comments filled Trent with rage, driven by emotion and without thinking, Trent drew his pistol and fired, killing Eli Strand instantly. Gaining control of himself, Trent quickly, jumped down off his horse, bent down over Eli's body and took his money pouch.

Trent had heard the same reports of bandits and Indians raiding along the Rio Grand, and Pecos River. Taking Eli's money pouch would make it look like any other robbery along the river. There was no reason for anyone to believe the killer was anyone other than a lone bandit.

Hearing the shot, Octavio came riding up from the river, only to see a lone rider racing away. By then the rider was too far away to identify.

The next year was extremely rough on Alejandra. She had a hard time coping with her father's death. Things were only made worse with the herd being depleted by rustlers. And to top everything else off, she now had an extra mouth to feed. A few weeks after her father's death, Octavio's daughter, Regina, showed up looking for a place to live after her mother passed away in Mexico City.

Regina was sixteen when she arrived at the ranch. Only a year younger than Alejandra, she was not nearly as experienced in life, and had no experience with living or working on a ranch. Instead of holding her upbringing against her, Alejandra embraced Regina and taught her how to read and speak English,. Of course, every day included lessons in horseback riding, shooting, and working the cattle. Regina embraced the hard life of working on a cattle ranch, even if it was in the dry hot Chihuahua desert. She and Alejandra became the very best of friends. In fact, they had grown as close as if they were sisters.

At the age of nineteen, it has been two years since Alejandra's father was murdered. She knew it was no longer possible to maintain the ranch and squeak out a living in the parched desert. She had wanted to quit on several occasions before, but felt obligated to provide for Octavio and Regina, something her father would have done. After considerable thought, she felt the time had finally come to sell the ranch and start over anew somewhere else. She instructed Octavio to harness the oxen to the Conestoga wagon and pack all their clothing and food. Then for him and Regina to round up the herd, which now consisted of only one hundred and twenty two longhorns.

"Octavio, I want you to be ready to pull out when I return."

Octavio was concerned about Alejandra and didn't understand what she was doing, or why they were rounding up the cattle.

"Where are we going Senorita?"

"Montana Territory!" She replied emphatically.

Still curious, he asked, "Where are you headed to now?"

"I am going to see Mr. Oswald and see if he will buy the ranch. He has been trying to make us give up for years, so I am going to give him the chance to be rid of us once and for all."

"What if he refuses?"

"We are going whether he purchases the ranch or not. This is the third straight year of drought, and we can't maintain the herd here any longer. Between the drought and rustlers, we have already lost over a third of the herd."

Octavio harnessed the oxen and was pulling the wagon out of the barn when Alejandra rode out to speak with Lucas Oswald, and offer to sell him the ranch. She went with little expectations, in fact she considered it a long shot that he would actually purchase the ranch.

Alejandra rode up to the Oswald house and dismounted. As she was tying her horse up to the hitch rail, Trent came out onto the porch and challenged her.

"To what do we owe the honor of a scrub rancher, like yourself, visiting the great Oswald ranch?"

"I wish to speak to your father Trent."

"Why don't you quit fighting the inevitable Alejandra, and accept my marriage proposal. I can provide you with everything you would ever want or need."

Holding nothing back she spoke in an even tone.

"Because you are a killer, and have no redeeming values. You couldn't offer me enough to even sit down to dinner with you, let alone marry you."

Trent raised his hand to strike Alejandra across the face when his father yelled at him.

"Trent!"

Lucas Oswald had come out onto the porch just in time to hear his son's words, and see him poised to strike Alejandra.

"Ms. Strand, I hope you will accept my apologies for my son's rude behavior."

"It's alright Mr. Oswald, I am use to him disrespecting me. I was hoping to have a word with you, alone, if I may."

"Please, step into the parlor, we can get out of the heat and enjoy a cool glass of lemonade as we talk."

Trent started to follow them into the house, when his father held out his arm, with his hand raised to block his advance.

"Trent, Ms. Strand and I will be speaking alone, as she has requested. You shall remain outside and respect her wishes."

After leading Alejandra inside and seating themselves in the parlor, Mr. Oswald spoke first.

"Please, tell me what it is you have on your mind young lady. It must be important for you to have ridden all the way over here in this heat."

"Mr. Oswald, you have been trying to get my father and me to sell out for the better part of fifteen years. The drought has taken its toll and I am no longer capable of sustaining the herd on the parched land.

Therefore, I am willing to sell you my ranch, but only the land and buildings, not the herd."

"If you don't mind my asking, what are your plans for the herd?"

"The herd is down to a hundred and twenty head, give or take a steer or two, and they are not in the best of shape. Lord knows you don't need them to enhance your herd. All the same, I will need them to start a new ranch elsewhere."

Trent had been listening just outside the door. Stepping into the parlor he spoke to his dad in an angry tone.

"Father, don't waste your money buying that wasteland they call a ranch. Hell, it will be ours for nothing in another year or two anyway."

His father snapped back.

"That's enough Trent, now leave us. I am sure there is work that requires your attention down at the barn."

Lucas Oswald knew what Trent had said was true. However, he felt guilt over the death of Alejandra's father. He knew it was his son, and not some lone bandit, who murdered her father. He found Eli Strand's money pouch hidden in Trent's room. Having seen the pouch on several occasions he recognized it as Eli's.

After a long silence, which Alejandra took as a bad sign, Mr. Oswald made an offer.

"How does ten thousand dollars sound?"

Alejandra could not believe what she had just heard.

"Mr. Oswald, that's ten dollars an acre. You know as well as I, that that scrub land isn't worth more than a dollar an acre."

"Does that mean you are declining my offer, Ms. Strand?"

"No sir, I accept your offer, and you have my greatest thanks."

Lucas smiled as he clasped both of her hands within his.

"No thanks is necessary my dear."

He couldn't bring Eli back to life, but in some small way, he thinks this helps make amends for his son killing Eli Strand. Still, Mr. Oswald was concerned with how his son might react to his offer.

"The sale is contingent on one thing Ms. Strand, you can not mention the sale price to anyone. If anyone should ask, merely state that we came to an equitable settlement. Most people will gather that means I purchased it cheap, and that you don't wish to embarrass yourself by disclosing the amount. There is no reason to upset Trent if we can help it. If he asks me, I will tell him I paid you $500, which is half of the amount you quoted me. That will make him happy. Besides, I can't have people spreading the word that a young lady out haggled me."

"You have my word sir, I will not disclose the amount of the sale."

Mr. Oswald was still curious as to her future plans.

"Where will you go now, if you don't mind disclosing where your headed?"

"I prefer to keep that a secret. As you said, there is no reason to disclose any information that could lead to trouble."

"Very well, I understand, and if I can be of any other support don't hesitate to contact me. I will keep Trent close to the ranch until you are well on your way."

After receiving the cash, Alejandra shook his hand and they said their goodbyes. Trent watched from the barn as she rode out, and quickly walked back to the house to speak with his father.

"Father, what did you pay her for that poor excuse of a ranch?"

"Five Hundred dollars, fifty cents an acre. It was worth it to finally be rid of the Strand ranch and obtain the access it provides to the Pecos River."

Trent understood and considered the $500 a bargain, knowing it was worth at least a dollar an acre. Even though he felt they would have eventually gotten it for nothing, he was satisfied that his dad purchased it at a bargain rate. Especially since it would further tie up the water rights along the Pecos River, which was worth far more than the land itself.

The next day Alejandra and Regina started pushing the herd and remuda of six horses north. Octavio followed in the wagon.

Chapter 4

Alejandra heard quite a bit about the wide open northern territories known as Montana, and also as the Indian Territory, with its tall grass, blue mountains, and never ending rivers. Diego Alejandro, Alejandra's uncle, had visited her and her father after returning from a cattle drive to the Montana Territory. He described it as the greenest and most beautiful place on earth. With thousands of acres just for the taking if you were willing to work hard and fight the Indians. Diego tried to talk Eli into moving there and starting over, to make a better life for himself and his daughter. After the death of his wife, Eli had no desire to move or start over. The risks and dangers involved with a cattle drive that far were more than he wished to face. Besides, Moving 1,500 miles north wasn't going to fill the void in his heart.

Alejandra understood the dangers involved with a trip of this magnitude, which she was about to embark upon. She estimated it would take no less than six months to drive the herd that far north. It would be a very difficult drive, even for the most seasoned cattlemen, let alone two women and an old man. They will have to battle rustlers, Indians, grizzlies, wolves, and arrive before winter set in. Worst of all she will have to contend with the land barons who think every piece of land adjacent to their boundaries belongs to them as well, both those on the trail and in the Montana Territory. Alejandra is no tender foot, she is as tough as they come. Not only in the areas most men consider tough, but also mentally.

The established ranchers will consider her an interloper and try to steal her ranch, claiming they have already staked claim to the land. True or not, they will brand her as a squatter and try to steal her herd. It is for this reason she has decided to build her ranch on Indian lands.

Her Uncle Diego mentioned the Crow were friendly with the white man. However, there was a limit to their acceptance of the whites, it only existed as long as the white man kept moving and didn't try to homestead on their lands, or try to capture their wild horses. Alejandra expects to use this knowledge and negotiate with the Crow, beef for land.

Winters in The Montana Territory are hard and food can be scarce. Her cattle can provide the Crow with much needed meat during the harsh winters when game is scarce. In return, she will be provided land and allowed to build her ranch within their territory. This will eliminate all property right disputes any of the current ranchers might be inclined to raise. And what better neighbors to have on her side than the Crow Nation.

After a week on the trail, they had driven the heard north about 80 miles, they were close to a place named Big Spring, Texas. It really wasn't a town, merely a campsite on the Overland Trail leading to California. The spring provided a water source for everyone, including the tribes of the Apache and Comanche Indians.

Alejandra and Regina would trade places riding drag and point everyday. Regina was riding drag when Alejandra rode back to talk to her.

"What's wrong, are we stopping here?"

" Nothing's wrong Regina, I place us about three miles out from Big Spring. I want to ride up ahead and check it out, make sure we aren't riding into Injun' trouble. I should rejoin you just before you reach the spring. I am having Octavio move the wagon up to the drag position so you can take the point. Regina, If Indians attack, abandon the herd, you and Octavio save yourselves."

Alejandra touched the spurs to her horse and cantered away, she disappeared from Regina's sight after about five minutes. Alejandra could see the smoke rising from the campfire about a half mile out from the spring. Keeping her horse in the soft sand to silence her approach, she walked him in the direction of the campfire. As she came to the outer edges of Big Spring, she rode into a stand of trees and dismounted. She didn't want to hail the camp until she could determine if they were friendly or not. Leaving her horse in the stand of trees she continued on foot. Shortly thereafter, she heard a woman crying. Based on the conversation, there were at least two, maybe three men, they were laughing and speaking in guttural voices.

Keeping under cover, she made her way up close to the camp and slipped in behind a large boulder unnoticed. On the edge of their camp, she could see the woman she heard crying. She was curled up on the ground naked, whimpering. Two men were standing over the woman. One with his pants down from having just raped the her, the other laughing.

Alejandra still wasn't certain if there were only the two men. Looking around, she couldn't see anyone other than the two men and the woman. She assumed their guttural sounds had amplified the noise to make it sound as if there might have been a third man.

Believing there were only the two, she drew her pistol and stepped out from behind the boulder. The two men raised their heads as one, and watched as she strolled into camp. They could see she was healed and pointing her pistol right at them. Seeing the gun, the man who had just finished raping the woman reached down to pull up his pants, the other one reached for his gun. The man's pistol was half way out of its holster when the bullet struck his hand, causing him to drop the pistol back into its holster.

"Step back gentlemen, and I use that term loosely. In case you're wondering, the answer is yes, I will kill you both if you make a wrong move. Don't underestimate me because I am a woman, I can shoot better than most men. You, the one holding his pant's up, collect her clothes and place them down next to her, then move back beside your partner."

The man did as he was told and Alejandra turned her attention to the woman.

"Ma'am, can you get dressed by yourself?"

"Yes, I'm not seriously hurt, just badly bruised and humiliated."

"What's your name, and how on earth did you end up with these two scoundrels?"

"My name is Melanie, most people call me Mel for short. My husband was killed by the Comanche while we were traveling through the Oklahoma Territory. These three buffalo hunters found me out on the prairie, and promised to take me the rest of the way to California to be with my relatives."

The cattle could smell the water and it was getting harder for Regina to hold them back from running to the spring. It had been more than two hours since Alejandra had left the herd. She was way overdue, and Regina was worried something bad has happened to her, or she was under attack by Indians.

Concerned Alejandra had run into trouble, Regina turned the herd to bed them down, then she rode back to the wagon.

"Dad, wait here with the herd. I need to ride up ahead and make sure Alejandra is safe."

Regina checked the loads in her pistol and rifle, saddled a fresh mount, then raced toward Big Springs.

Alejandra instantly realized her mistake when Melanie said *"three"* hunters. Before she could react, she heard the hammer of a pistol cock behind her as the man said, "freeze".

With his pistol pointed at Alejandra's back, the man spoke to one of his companions.

"What's goin' on here Iggy, why is this woman holdin' a pistol on you and Lester?"

"Marquis, I told Lester not to touch that woman like you said, but he just had to have her. He was pullin' his pants up when this bitch showed up shootin'."

"What's your interest in this woman little lady? You some kind of kin or somethin'?"

Alejandra kept her pistol aimed at the other two as she answered the man holding a gun on her back.

"She is a helpless woman being raped by a filthy dog. That makes it my business."

"Watch your mouth lady, that's my brother your talkin' about. What brings you out here to the middle of nowhere anyway?"

"I am moving a herd to Montana."

"If you're moving a herd, then why haven't I seen a dust cloud or herd them bawlin'? Just how far out is this herd?"

"Approximately three miles out."

That was how far out they were when she left the herd. She knew they should be within a half mile of the spring by now, but Marquis was right, if the cattle were that close they should be hearing them bawl.

"Well, it's just your bad luck, showin' up when you did little lady. You know I can't let you live to report my brother rapin' that there woman. Settlers don't take kindly to molestin' a woman out here on the plains. They would hang him for certain, if not all of us."

"I hope your fast, because your brothers are going to be dead before I fall."

"That's the only reason I haven't shot you yet. I don't believe you could get them both, but you might get lucky and kill one of them. In any case, I don't wish to lose either one of them."

Not concerning herself with her own plight, Alejandra inquired about Melanie.

"What about her, you going to shoot her too, or just use her to pleasure yourselves some more before dumping her in the desert without food or water?"

"She'll have to die too. But like you said, not until we have had some more fun with the both of you. Who knows, if you treat us extra special, maybe we'll let you live. Now, drop that pistol and slide out of those buckskins. I imagine a young little filly like yourself is prob'ly still a virgin."

Alejandra was not about to drop her pistol. If she was going to die she was going to go out fighting. Just as she was about to turn and fire, Regina worked the action on her rifle, sending a bullet into the chamber and cocking the hammer. Then spoke loud and clear.

"That's good advice mister, drop your gun."

Spinning on her boot heels, Alejandra closed the distance between her and Marquis, and snatched the pistol out of his hand. At the same time, she pressed the barrel of her own pistol hard into his chest.

Alejandra's anger had been building up in her for letting Marquis sneak up behind her, and it has now reached the boiling point. She hated these men for what they had done to Melanie. She began pulling up the slack on the trigger.

Regina was watching her and knew she would shoot him if she didn't intervene.

"He ain't worth it Alejandra."

"Maybe not, but it would sure make me feel a whole lot better knowing he won't waylay any more trusting or unsuspecting women. Regina, go get the herd and bring them up to the spring. We won't be spending the night here, there is a lake two miles north of here where we can stop for the night. Mel, grab Iggy and Lester's pistols and keep them covered. Can you do that and shoot them if they move?"

"Yes, my husband taught me how to shoot a pistol during our travels overland. At this range I will not miss."

Regina returned with the herd and moved them to the springs to water. Alejandra had staked out the three men. She wasn't satisfied with just staking them out though, she made them strip first, so they could feel the same humiliation they put Melanie through. Lastly, using a burning stick from the campfire, she had carved the word "Rapist" across Lester's chest.

After the herd finished watering, they started them north. It was a struggle to get the herd moving again. With the sun setting and having just filled their bellies with water, all they wanted to do was lie down and chew their cud. They arrived at the lake two miles north of the springs not long after sundown. With the threat of the buffalo hunters breaking their bonds, and Indians in the area, Alejandra decided it would be best to ride night herd. Something they had not done up until now. Mostly because of their limited manpower and the small remuda of horses. Alejandra and Regina put in a hard day's work each day keeping the herd together, so they opted to sleep instead of riding night herd. Besides after being on the trail all day, all the cattle wanted to do was lie down and sleep. There was no worry of them drifting off.

Alejandra divided the night herd duties between the three of them. Because of the late hour and Alejandra wanting to get an early start, each one of them only had to stand a two hour shift. Octavio took the middle shift so the women could each get a longer uninterrupted sleep.

Alejandra gave Mel the opportunity to join them on their adventure north to Montana, and become a part of their small family. If she didn't, Alejandra promised to find her transport west to join her family in California. There was no hesitation on Mel's part, she immediately accepted Alejandra's offer to join them on their trek north.

As was true with most frontier women, Mel was an excellent cook, much better than any of the others. Since she was not very good riding a horse, she had to ride drag. Tough duty for anyone, let alone a thirty five year old woman, but she didn't complain. She was happy to be traveling with her new found friends. Whom she felt safe with after they rescued her from a terrible fate. This was her family now, and she had no intention of leaving, regardless of how hard the work.

Alejandra took the buffalo hunters horses, and two mules loaded down with buffalo hides. She also kept their rifles, pistols, and skinning knifes. Even if those men survived the desert heat, wild animals, or Indians, which she doubted, she didn't want them armed and following them seeking retribution. Neither did she want to leave them with any weapons to prey on other unsuspecting folks.

Alejandra knew they would need the hides themselves to help weather the cold Montana winters. The extra mounts were a significant help also, allowing them to rest a third of the remuda now on a rotating basis.

With no way of knowing, the Apache arrived at the spring not long after they had moved on. They scalped the buffalo hunters, and sliced open their bellies, releasing their entrails for the animals and insects to eat while the men were still alive. Albeit not for long.

Some weeks later, having traveled well into the Unorganized Territory, they came across the El Pueblo trading post, located in the Arkansas River Valley. Needing to restock their supplies, Alejandra decided to stop and let the cattle graze. Leaving Regina and Octavio with the herd on Fountain Creek, she took Mel along with her in the wagon down to the trading post.

While putting together their supplies, a girl no older than fifteen came stumbling out of the back room. A large man was pawing her and laughing. The girl twisted in an attempt to pull away from him. It was obvious by the owners reaction that she was being prostituted. Her facial lines indicated she was half Indian. The owner made a light protest for the man to let the girl go, unless he wanted to pay for more time. The man grunted his disapproval and after letting her go he left.

Alejandra moved to the girl's side while continuing to look over the goods set out for sale. Without raising too much suspicion she spoke to her.

The girl told her that after her parents deaths, the proprietor of the trading post who had been a good friend of her father, took her in and gave her a place to live. He had promised her father that he would provide and take care of her. A year after her fathers death, he started using her as a whore to pay for her keep, and then some.

"What is your name?" Alejandra asked.

"I am Skah, it's Sioux for white. Pronounced "Skaw" by the Sioux, but "Sky" by most white people. My mother was a Lakota and named me for my father being a white man."

"Sky, would you like to leave this place and live free again?"

"You don't know how often I have thought about running away. But he would chase me down and bring me back. Besides, where would I go and how would I live?"

"I am moving a herd to the Montana Territory. You are welcome to come with us. All we ask is that you pull your own weight and share equally in the work. If you would like to join us, go pack your belongings. When you see us loading our last bundle, walk out and climb into the back of the wagon."

As Sky walked past the counter with her small carpet bag, Boone ran out from behind the counter and chased her out the door.

"Stop! Where do you think you're going? You belong to me until your debt is paid."

Just as Boone was about to grab Sky, Alejandra drew her pistol and fired a shot at his feet.

"Lay a hand on her and I will kill you."

"She is my property, I can do with her as I please."

"She is the daughter of the man you once called a friend. Do you think he would have brought her here if he knew you would turn her into a prostitute? She is not your property, and is free to come and go as she chooses. If you have any objections to her leaving, you can settle your dispute with me, here and now."

"I am not heeled, you'd shoot me in cold blood?"

"For enslaving a young girl, and selling her to the trappers that come and go for your own gain, you bet I would."

"Take her then, and don't come back through these parts again if you know what's good for you."

Alejandra had a suspicion the fight for Sky wasn't over. It was likely Boone was making more money off her than he was making selling liquor and supplies.

After supper Alejandra and Regina slipped out into the rocks to guard the camp. It was just past midnight when Boone and another man came riding into their camp, yelling and firing their pistols into the air.

Alejandra and Regina's shots found their marks. Causing a different kind of yell from the men as they drop their pistols to the ground. Boone had thought it would be easy to ride in and scare a wagon full of women. He learned the hard way, that just because they were women, they weren't defenseless.

Alejandra yelled down from behind the rocks.

"Boone, I told you what I'd do if you didn't leave Sky alone."

Boone started stuttering.

"P-P-Please, don't s-s-shoot us. I am s-sorry, you can leave and take her with you. I won't cause any more t-t-trouble, I promise."

Alejandra moved down from the rocks to face Boone and his henchman. Pointing her pistol at Boone's head as if to shoot him, Alejandra spoke sternly.

"Both of you, remove your boots, pants and shirts."

After doing as they were told, the two men stood there facing her in their long johns, shaking from the fear of being killed. Alejandra merely thought they were shivering from the cold. Had she known it was from fear of being shot, she might have had a little fun with them.

Although she felt they deserved to die, for prostituting a young helpless girl, Alejandra had no desire to kill them. So she gave them their marching orders and sent them on their way.

"Now, You two turn around and start walking. If you return again I will not be so forgiving."

Boone didn't know when to shut up and accept defeat.

"What about our horses and guns?"

Just as cool as any gunfighter, Alejandra looked Boone directly in the eyes.

"They belong to me now. If you would like to challenge me for them, I am willing to give you one more chance. If you can beat me to the draw, you can take your belongings, with the exception of Sky. If not you will be dead and it won't matter."

Boone turned without saying another word and pushed his partner to start walking in front of him. He knew he wasn't up to the task. Even though she was a woman, Boone knew he would have been killed if he had tried to brace her with a gun. The two men headed back to the trading post. With any luck they would make it back to the post somewhere around noon. That was if the Indians or wolves didn't get them first.

Once again, without having a mind to, they had increased their remuda and arsenal by adding the guns and horses of Boone and his partner.

It turned out Sky is an excellent rider, not quite as proficient with a pistol as Alejandra or Regina, but a dead shot with a rifle. As good as either Alejandra or Regina, which was saying a lot. Her father was a mountain man who taught her to shoot and hunt with a .54 caliber Sharps Breech loading rifle. There were several occasions during the drive that Sky used her hunting skills to provide meat. This kept them from having to butcher any of their small herd for survival.

It was July of 1852, when they arrived in the upper part of the Bighorn Valley in Montana. It didn't take Alejandra long to develop a strong friendship with the Crow. They allowed her to stake out ten thousand acres of land in Crow territory to build her ranch. In exchange for the land she would provide them with beef during the winters.

In addition, the Crow agreed to help protect the ranch against attack from the Sioux and Blackfoot. The Flathead and Shoshone lands also bordered the Crow lands to the north and west, but they rarely crossed over into Crow lands or caused trouble. The Sioux and Blackfoot were constantly raiding the Crow's horse herds.

With just over a hundred head of cattle, the others questioned Alejandra's judgment for staking out so much land. She informed them that it was her objective to be one of the largest, if not the largest, cattle ranch in the territory.

With lush rolling grass meadows, the ranch sat in the basin where the Bighorn and Yellowstone rivers converged. Alejandra chose the place well, and made sure they would always have access to plenty of water. She didn't want a repeat of what happened in Texas with the Oswald's controlling access to the water.

This was Crow territory, and as far as she knew, they were the only whites allowed to settle inside the basin. Other than hers, there were only a couple large ranches in the area. One to the west and the other to the south, but they were far enough apart not to dispute one another's property lines or grazing rights. Besides, to challenge her was to challenge the Crow. Otherwise, there were several small ranches, each measuring about 640 acres, known as a full section.

All the stock and supplies were furnished by Alejandra, even so, she decided to share the ownership of the ranch between herself and the other three women, and Octavio. She retained fifty one percent ownership for herself, she gave Octavio and Regina twenty nine percent as they had been with her originally, and worked the ranch in Texas. Mel and Sky were given ten percent each. They were all overjoyed with Alejandra's generosity. She owed them nothing, with the exception of Octavio who had been with her father before she was born. In fact, in one way or another, they all owed their lives to her. The only provision placed upon them, was that if any of them decided to leave, the ownership rights would be sold back to Alejandra and to no one else.

The first order of business was to construct the three main buildings, a ranch house, bunkhouse, and barn with an attached corral and holding pens. With the vast pastures and water, the cattle wouldn't venture very far. Even if they did, they would most likely still be on the Ranch.

The ranch house was built large enough to house all four women and included a guest room, parlor, and dining room. With a breezeway between it and an attached kitchen. The bunkhouse, for Octavio and the ranch hands to come was built next, followed by the barn. They decided to name the ranch in a way that included all four women. So they took the first letter of each woman's name, and based upon their arrival into the fold, the "ARMS Ranch" was born. "A" for Alejandro, "R" for Regina, "M" for Melanie, and "S" for Sky.

Chapter 5

The Sioux have been raiding inside Crow lands more of late, stealing cattle and horses. The gold rush has brought increased numbers of white men. As a result, the buffalo, deer and elk populations were being depleted, making it difficult for the Sioux to feed their families. Not to mention, the white people were now homesteading on Sioux lands instead of passing through to the great western water. They were in great need of horses to fight the large wagon trains, and to cover longer distances quickly.

Unfortunately, the raids against the Crow have placed the ARMS Ranch at risk. The ranch is located in between the Sioux and Crow nations.

Alejandra and Regina, along with three ranch hands, were riding the southeast section of the ranch looking for any sign of a Sioux raiding party. That's when they heard the shots. Spurring their horses, they rode in the direction the shots came from, thinking the Crow were under attack. To their surprise, they saw a band of five Sioux chasing a single white man who was trailing three horses. The next thing they saw was the man falling out of his saddle. No doubt the result of the three arrows sticking out of his body.

Even from a distance Alejandra could see the beauty of the man's horses. He laid motionless in the grass, making it difficult to determine if he was alive or dead. She could see at least two arrows sticking out of him. Regardless, alive or not, if they didn't react quickly, he would be dead for sure, and those horses would be lost forever. Leading the way she gave the order to give chase and retrieve those stolen horses. After a furious running gun battle, lasting less than five minutes, and resulting in the death of three Sioux, the two remaining braves released their hold on the stolen horses and fled.

Alejandra was still barking out orders.

"Grayson, take Jason and Devon, and round up those horses. Regina, you come with me, we'll check on the downed cowboy."

Alejandra dismounted to check on the wounded cowboy to determine if he was still alive. Aside from the arrows, the first thing Alejandra noticed was how handsome the young man was, and that he looked to be her approximate age.

Regina was looking down as she sat atop her horse.

"What do you think Alejandra, will he live?"

"I think if we don't get him back to the ranch and get these arrows out of him he will die for sure. Even then, I don't give him much of a chance."

As she was talking to Regina, Grayson and the others rode up trailing the man's horses.

"Grayson, you and Devon take the horses to the barn and bring back a wagon. We need to get this gunfighter back to the ranch. Wait, I want to get a better look at the brand on those horses."

It was a very unusual Brand, made up of a horse head with a flowing mane and the initial "K" set inside the neck line. She wondered if any of her hands were familiar with the brand.

"Any of you ever seen this brand before?"

All three shook their heads no, indicating they hadn't seen it before.

"Alright, get moving and hurry back with that wagon."

She called him a gunfighter, but why, she held the thought to herself. *"Why did I call him a gunfighter, was it because of his tied down guns, set low on his waist? He isn't dressed like a cowpuncher or stockman, so where did he get those beautiful horses? Did he steal them? Is that why he's traveling alone this far north through Indian territory? Did he steal that string of horses and come here to escape the law?"*

All unanswered questions, but most of all, he brought back memories of Trent Oswald. Who although handsome, intelligent, and brought up in wealth, turned into a cold blooded killer.

Still thinking to herself. *"I am embarrassed, that even at a time like this, I find myself attracted to this man. I can't help but wonder though if this man is made from the same cloth as Trent Oswald?"*

Regina interrupted Alejandra's personal thoughts.

"Alejandra, we can't wait until we get him back to the ranch, we have to get those arrows out of him now."

"I know Regina, but I'm not sure he is worth saving. He looks like a gunfighter to me, and he is probably a horse thief to boot."

"Alejandra, what's wrong with you. You aren't sounding like yourself. You have always shown compassion for others, what is it that makes this man so different that he deserves your mistrust?"

"He reminds me of Trent, but you're right, he needs our help. Jason, step down and give me a hand."

Trying not to cause the man any further injury, Jason rolled Corey over onto his side so they could see if the arrows passed all the way through. The arrows had entered his back as he rode away from his attackers. One was sticking out the center of his back, but fortunately had not penetrated through his heart, the second one hit him in his lower back passing all the way through his front, while the third arrow penetrated all the way through his thigh. Other than contributing to the blood loss, the lower back and thigh wounds were not life threating.

Alejandra broke off the arrowheads of those arrows penetrating all the way through his lower back and thigh. Then, instructing Jason to hold him tight and not to let him move, she pulled the two arrows out. The man remained unconscious and never felt the pain of the arrows being removed. She couldn't take the chance on pulling the arrow out of the center of his back without killing him.

"We can't do anymore for him out here, Regina. We have to get him back so Octavio can remove this last arrowhead."

She broke off the arrow at the base of the skin. Not having any bandages, she reached into her saddle bags and withdrew the extra shirt she always carried. Then cut out some patches to plug the open wounds and slow the bleeding.

Corey was still unconscious when they arrived back at the ranch. Octavio was able to cut the arrowhead out without causing any further damage. Mel dressed all the wounds with local herbs she had harvested.

Over the past five years Mel had learned quite a bit from the Indians about the local herbs and their healing properties, for fighting infections and illness. As the mother figure of the group, she just naturally took on the doctoring responsibilities, along with being the chief cook.

Corey lost so much blood it was a struggle to survive. Mel cared for him day and night to make sure he pulled through. Four days passed before Corey regained consciousness. Squinting to see, he tried to get his bearings, nothing seemed familiar. He saw the woman sitting at the table in the middle of the room and tried to speak, but his words were garbled due to his dry mouth and swollen throat.

Mel heard him mumble and quickly moved to his side. Careful not to choke him she gave him small amounts of water. After quenching his initial thirst, he slipped back off to sleep, that was when Mel ran to tell Alejandra he was awake.

Hearing the news, everyone rushed down to the bunkhouse. Mel was the last to arrive, she had went to the kitchen and taken the time to make a small bowl of hot broth. Corey had awakened again during Mel's absence and was startled when Alejandra and the others came crashing through the door. Alejandra was firing one question after another at him, not waiting for a rely before asking the next. His speech was slow and labored, but he managed to say his name, "Corey Kittridge"; then kept repeating the phrase, "My horses, where are my horses?"

Corey had not asked about his health, he was more concerned about those horses than his own life. The concern he showed for the horses convinced Alejandra he wasn't a horse thief. No horse thief would have been more concerned about the horses he stole than his own life.

Alejandra was irritated by how Regina and Sky were fawning all over the cowboy, although she couldn't understand why she was feeling so irritated. After all, he was a drifter and meant nothing to her. As he started to fade out again, Mel chased everyone out so he could rest.

Over the next month Corey regained most of his strength, and his wounds left no ill effect, other than some ugly scars. Having fully recuperated, he was feeling well enough to move on. The problem was, he owed Alejandra his life, and with winter setting in fast, he wasn't prepared to build his own ranch. The snows were coming, and he had no supplies set in to survive the winter.

It was a nice cool fall morning, but Corey found himself sweating as he walked up to the house. He couldn't understand why he was perspiring so profusely. Grayson greeted him on the porch. After tipping his hat back to wipe his brow, Corey returned the greeting.

"Good morning Grayson, I wish to speak with Alejandra if she is available."

"She'll be right out."

Alejandra had been watching Corey from the parlor as he walked up from the bunkhouse. She stepped out onto the porch and Cory removed his hat to greet her.

"Ma'am, I wanted to thank you for saving my life. To show my appreciation, I would like to present you one of my Andalusian mares. I know it can never make up for all you've done for me, but the horses are all I own. It would please me very much if you would accept a mare of your choosing."

Alejandra was overwhelmed by Corey's generosity, and before she could refuse the offer, Jason came walking up with the three mares.

"I am sorry I can't offer you the stallion, but I need him for stud to get my horse ranch started. I trust you'll understand and forgive my selfishness."

A tear came to Alejandra's eye as she responded to Corey's generous offer.

"The pollen is really making my eyes water this morning. I would be proud to accept one of your mares as a gift, and I fully understand your not being able to part with your stallion."

Stepping down off the porch, she carefully inspected each mare, although there was no need, she knew they were all of equal quality. She was just using the time to gain her composer before speaking again. Alejandra was thinking to herself as she walked between the mares. *"These horses are all he has and he is willing to give one to me. After I had harbored such horrible thoughts of disrespect against him. Even if he didn't know about my thoughts, he was well aware of my aloofness and the poor attitude I exhibited towards him during his recuperation. For the last month I have thought the worst of him, considering him a ruthless gunfighter and possible horse thief."*

Although still of great stature, she selected the smallest mare, wanting him to keep the larger ones for breeding.

"Thank you so very much Corey, I don't know what to say or how to thank you for your generosity."

Corey quickly responded.

"Ma'am, there is something you can do for me. Winter is only a few weeks away and I have missed too much time to search for land, and build proper shelters for myself and my horses. I would very much appreciate it if you would let me stay on here and work as the horse wrangler over the winter. I promise to work as hard as if it were my own ranch."

Alejandra's heart filled with emotion, she didn't understand the feeling she was having at this very moment, but for whatever reason, she was extremely happy he had found a means of remaining on the ranch.

"Yes, Mr. Kittridge you are more than welcome to remain on the ARMS Ranch, and you may stay as long as you desire, or find necessary. Speak with my Foreman, Mr. Grayson, he will make sure you have whatever you require for managing our horses."

Maybe Alejandra didn't understand the emotions flowing through her body, but Regina and Sky knew exactly what she was feeling. They had been watching her from the window the whole time. It was obvious Alejandra was in love with Mr. Kittridge. This explained her poor attitude towards him and not allowing herself to get close to him.

Over the next two months, Corey rode over the entire ranch. Today he was riding the northwest corner of the ranch looking for wild horses, when he came across a band of Crow. One of the Crow understood and spoke English and translated for him. They had seen him riding the hills, but wasn't aware he was working for the ARMS Ranch. Corey was surprised when the translator introduced Acaraho, Chief of the Crow.

They dismounted and sat for some time talking about nothing but horses. Acaraho was impressed with

Corey's knowledge of horses. Before leaving, Corey had struck a bargain with Acaraho to catch wild horses for the Crow. In exchange he would receive land to build his ranch. The agreement also included Corey getting to select a Stallion and five mares from each group of horses numbering twenty or more.

Corey was not oblivious to the unrest between the whites and the Sioux. It would only be a matter of time before horses would be in great demand by the Army, which was sure to come to the territory to protect the miners and pioneers. It would be a couple years from now, but he needed that time to build up his herds.

Five months have past since Corey became the horse wrangler on the ARMS Ranch. It was now March and Corey had never worked so hard. It has been difficult for him to manage his time between the job as horse wrangler for the ARMS Ranch, catching wild horses for Acaraho, and cutting timber to build his own cabin and barns.

Alejandra kept a close eye on Corey as he worked around the ranch. She couldn't help but admire him for his work ethic. He never neglected his duties on the ARMS Ranch to work on his own place, or catch wild horses. In fact, he had never mentioned anything other than ARMS Ranch business to Alejandra, he specifically kept quiet about his private endeavors of catching wild horses and cutting timber.

It was Acaraho that told her about Corey building his own ranch and catching wild horses for the Crow. Otherwise, she wouldn't have known. No matter how hard she tried to ignore him, it wasn't working. In fact, it was just the opposite, she found herself being drawn toward him more and more each day. Probably the reason she continued keeping a close eye on him. It had nothing to do with his work, that was only an excuse for her to be close and talk to him.

Over the long winter, when Corey wasn't chasing horses or working on his own ranch, Corey spoke to the other hands in the bunkhouse of his dream to build his own horse ranch. Corey had become a good friend and saddle partner to Jason. It was to him that Corey spoke most with about his new ranch, and his past in Texas. They rode the ranch together most every day.

Apart from what Acaraho told her, Alejandra learned more about Corey's horse ranch from Regina. That was because Regina and Jason were having a romance, and of course what he told her she would pass on to Alejandra.

Chapter 6

Corey's father was a noted horse trainer in England and worked for a British Nobleman. When King George took over the country in 1820, times were very dangerous and the Nobleman gave his father a breeding pair of Spanish Andalusian horses, and paid his passage to America for the loyalty he had displayed.

After migrating to America, Corey's father, Matthew Kittridge, worked his way across the country from New York to Eagle Creek, a small Mexican community in the plateaus of northern Mexico along the Canadian River. Eagle Creek, along with most of the northeast portion of Mexico above the Rio Grand, became part of the Republic of Texas in 1836.

Matthew knew he could not survive raising horses alone, so he and the three Vaquero's that worked for him headed south to the Nueces River, where they rounded up 200 wild longhorns. They were plentiful and free for the taking if you had the courage and strength to capture them. They took a remuda of thirty six horses, of which they each used four horses a day to work the cattle. The roundup was immensely difficult, the cattle were mean and stubborn from free ranging for so long. The longhorns would charge the horses trying to hook them with their horns. It took the four men over two months to round them up, working sunup to sundown. The fact that the cattle didn't venture far from the river helped. They selected the ten best bulls and released the rest.

All the horses in the remuda were Mustangs with the exception of the two Andalusia's Matthew brought from England. Matthew used them to get the toughest longhorns out of the cedar breaks. The Vaqueros were astonished at the strength and speed of the Andalusia's.

Not to mention their courage in the face of a charging bull.

Corey was born in May of 1832. His mother died from typhoid fever when he was twelve. Initially all they had to worry about were the Comanche. It was the persistent raids by the Comanche that kept most Anglos and Mexicans from settling in the northern section of Mexico and Republic of Texas. Although Mexico never recognized the Republic, it never maintained much of a presence in that area. Most of Mexico's residents were established in the Sante Fe area.

That all changed after Texas was granted Statehood in 1845. The most notable change being the arrival of the Vance brothers, Tyrone and Forest, to Eagle Creek. They were arrogant and determined to own the largest ranch in the area and control the cattle market. To do so they would have to take possession of the many small ranches. Most of which were owned by Mexicans who had lived in and around Eagle Creek their whole lives.

The ranchers that refused to sell out at a price below value, Tyrone forced to leave by other means. Some just disappeared, and it was widely believed Tyrone killed them, or had them killed.

Tyrone fancied himself a gunfighter, and didn't hesitate to force his will on others. Forest was more passive and spent most of his time managing the business side of the ranch. Forest didn't approve of Tyrone's methods, but he remained silent about the tactics employed by Forest and his gunmen. Mostly because it served their purpose in running off the small ranchers so they could lay claim to their property and herds.

The Kittridge Ranch was probably the largest ranch in the area before the Vance brothers arrived. They had a herd of longhorns numbering over eight hundred now, along with over two hundred head of horses. Corey's father had been selling beef and horses to the army under a gentleman's agreement. He saw no need for a written contract.

All the ranches in the area sold beef and horses to the army under a gentleman's agreement. No one ranch tried to monopolize the market. This allowed all the ranchers and the town to prosper. It also eliminated the need for one rancher to overgraze his lands in an effort to supply the Army with all of its cattle and horses.

The Vance brothers entered into an exclusive contract with the Army to provide all their cattle and beef. Not only was it simpler to purchase its beef and horses from one ranch, but the Army received a discount from the Vance Ranch based on the volume of sales.

It wasn't long after the Vance brothers entered their agreement as the sole provider of stock to the Army, that the cattle rustling began. The Indians stole small amounts of cattle for food, but never large portions of a herd. While no one could prove it, everyone knew it was Tyrone Vance behind the cattle and horse rustling. The two ranchers who verbally expressed this belief were shot and killed by Tyrone. They were goaded into a gun fight by Tyrone, but because the ranchers drew first, the law classified the killings as self defense.

The Kittridge ranch had been hit hard, and many of Matthews ranch hands returned to Mexico fearing they would be shot. One night Matthew Kittridge and five ranch hands were killed protecting the herd from cattle rustlers. All the cattle and horses were stolen, with the exception of the Andalusian stallion and three mares Corey was training. It was only because they were stabled in the barn that night that they were not taken with the rest of the herd. The next morning Corey rode out to see why his father hadn't returned. Matthew Kittridge lived just long enough to tell his son that Tyrone Vance and his hired guns stole the herds and killed him and his Vaqueros.

Corey was not a mean person, and unknown to everyone other than his father, and a few other ranch hands, he had become very skilled at the fast draw. Corey rode into town and dismounted in front of the Brass Rail Saloon. Tyrone and two of his gunmen were standing at the bar drinking when Corey stepped through the batwing doors. He remembers the event clearly and replays it in his mind every day. He started speaking softly to Tyrone, so as not to let his anger control his actions.

"Tyrone, I am here to kill you for murdering my father and our Vaqueros, and rustling our herds."

All three men turned to brace him, although it was Tyrone who spoke.

"Boy you need to turn around and walk out of here before you die."

Without notice, the two men standing at the sides of Tyrone drew to fire. Corey had been ready and when they went for their guns he drew and fired two shots. Both men were dead and falling to the floor as Corey re-holstered his pistol.

Tyrone was impressed with Corey's speed and accuracy.

"That was pretty quick kid, I had no idea you were so fast with a gun. But those two were no where close to being as fast as I am."

Regardless of Tyrone's boast, and how confident he was about beating Corey to the draw, the concern about what he had just witnessed clearly showed on his face. He preferred to catch Corey unaware at some other place and time. Somewhere more to his liking, such as a blind bend in the road.

"Kittridge, I am going to give you one last chance to leave this saloon alive."

Corey was disgusted with Tyrone's cavalier attitude toward the death of his father, and his believing he was better than everyone else.

"I think I'll stay and finish what I've started."

Tyrone's hand flashed to his gun, but just as he was clearing leather, Corey fired two rounds into his chest. The gun slipped from Tyrone's hand, unaware to Corey, Tyrone's last thought was; *"How could I have been bested by this young kid."*

The men who saw the shooting all testified that Tyrone and his men all went for their guns first. So as the sheriff had done previously, with Tyrone's killings before, he declared the killings as self defense. Corey returned to his ranch, knowing the law was satisfied and no further action would be taken. However, the next day, Forest Vance exerted his influence over the Commanding Officer at the Fort, convincing him to force the sheriff into arresting Corey for the murder of his brother.

Not comfortable with the injustice being dished out as a result of Forest Vance's influence, the remaining ranchers gathered up Corey's stallion and three mares, and broke him out of jail. Convinced by the other ranchers it was no longer safe for him to stay in Texas, Corey gathered up the reins to his horse and headed north to The Montana Territory.

Chapter 7

As Regina told Alejandra the story of Corey's father being murdered, and Corey's retribution killing of Forest Vance and his two henchmen, Alejandra's legs weakened. It so reminded her of her own father's fate. She sat down before her legs gave out completely and she fell down. She understood why Corey had killed those men. She had long wished she knew who murdered her father, so she could have avenged him as Corey had avenged his father.

Alejandra's feelings for Corey continued to grow every day. Not only had Corey given her one of his magnificent Andalusia's, a gift greater than any she had ever received before, he continually showed himself to be considerate and kind. Far different than her initial suspicion of him being a gunfighter and thief. The story she had just heard buried those thoughts forever.

Regina reminded Alejandra how important it was to keep this knowledge of Corey's past a secret. Not only because it would place Corey in danger because he was wanted for murder, but because Corey had told it to Jason in secret. Regina didn't want Jason upset with her for betraying his confidence. Alejandra promised to keep the secret.

With spring having arrived, Corey knows the time has arrived to move on and start his own ranch. He saw Alejandra and Regina talking on the porch of the main house. There was no reason to put it off any longer, so he stepped into the saddle and walked "Spirit", his stallion, over to the porch. Feeling uncomfortable with having to give the news of his leaving, he remained mounted to stay steadfast.

"Alejandra, I wish to thank you and your friends once again for saving my life, and giving me a place to live and work throughout the winter months. Spring has arrived and it's time for me to leave and start building my own place. As you may know by now, Chief Acaraho has granted me a parcel of land northeast of here on the other side of the Bighorn River."

Alejandra was having trouble containing her emotions. Now that he was leaving, she finally understood the feelings she'd been having for him all along. She was in love with him, and didn't want him to leave in fear she would lose him forever.

"Corey, aren't you happy living here?"

"Yes Ma'am, but I have my own life to live and ranch to build."

"We would like very much for you to stay. You can continue to work here as horse wrangler. In addition, I will allow you to take whatever time away from work you need to work on your own ranch buildings. Isn't there anything I can do or say to change your mind?"

Alejandra was close to tears knowing he would be leaving, regardless of how hard she pleaded. She just couldn't find the courage to tell him she loved him. Had she done so Corey may never have left.

"You have been very kind to me, and I have enjoyed working here, but it is important that I establish a place of my own. I will stop by and visit you from time to time, and you are more than welcome to visit my place any time you would like."

Corey was feeling sorrow having to leave, because he had fallen in love with Alejandra. He wheeled Spirit around before his innards' erupted from the sickness he felt at having to leave her and his newly formed friends behind. As with Alejandra, he could not find the courage to tell her how he felt about her.

Collecting his two remaining mares, Corey left, looking back just before slipping out of sight to wave goodbye. Alejandra ran into the house and upstairs to her bedroom so no one would see her crying.

Corey's ranch was only fifteen miles northeast of the ARMS Ranch main compound . As he rode up to what would become the Kittridge Ranch, his new home, he found his herd of wild horses still grazing in the small canyon where he had put them. The canyon made a natural pasture, with lush grass and a spring fed stream for water. All he had to do was construct a pole fence to close off the canyon entrance. It was just outside this canyon with the river at his back that Corey decide to erect the main buildings for his ranch.

He put his Andalusia's in the pole corral he had already built, and that will eventually become a part of the barn arena. After feeding and watering the horses, Corey rolled up a cut stump and sat down to look over his new place. He sighed with a feeling of self satisfaction.

Corey's father taught him everything he knew about breeding and training horses. All that needed to be done now was to put in the hard work, something Corey never shied away from.

Corey was able to talk two young Crow braves into coming to work for him. They had helped him trap horses on a couple of occasions and they considered him a great horseman. Initially the two merely stood guard on the horses to prevent the Sioux from stealing them.

Corey made a trip up into the Saskatchewan Province of Canada to purchase a couple draft horses from the French colony. The mustangs have staying power when it comes to riding all day, but they lacked the power and stamina of the draft horses that he required for clearing the land and hauling logs.

The two Crow were critical in helping Corey build the houses and barn. Even though they were mostly just an extra pair of hands to hold and place the logs atop one another while Corey set them into place. By the time summer arrived, the ranch house, barn and bunkhouse had all been completed. The two Crow were now well accustomed to the English versions of their Indian names, Panther and Bear, that Corey called them.

During the evening hours, they would sit around the fire and teach one another the other's language. While not proficient in either's language, they were now capable of communicating without much difficulty. This would change as Panther and Bear became more proficient at speaking and understanding English. As was the case with Corey and the Crow language, in addition to his learning a little Sioux.

Regina and Jason rode over to see Corey twice during the Spring. Corey asked why Alejandra had not yet come by to see his ranch. Regina told him that Alejandra missed him, and that he should ride over to visit her. That she wouldn't admit her feelings for him and was too stubborn to make the first gesture. Regina was befuddled at how stubborn they were both being about expressing their feelings for one another.

"Maybe later in the summer. Right now I have to capture some more horses and get them broke before summer's end. With any luck I will be able to double my herd with new foals early next year."

Regina couldn't understand Corey's desire for a horse ranch.

"Horses, why aren't you raising cattle? There is a greater need for beef to eat, than horses to ride."

"That may be true for now, but the army will be here before long. The miners and pioneers are already demanding protection from the Sioux. The Army will be in need of horses, and I intend on selling them all the mounts they need."

Jason Scoffed, "You are such a dreamer."

"Maybe so Jason, but it is a dream my father and I shared, and one I intend on making a reality."

By summers end Corey had captured over three hundred mustangs, half of which he gave to Chief Acaraho. Panther and Bear had proven to be excellent horsemen themselves, and learned quickly from Corey. Between the three of them, they gentle broke all but a few of the two hundred plus horses that made up Corey's herd. As for the Andalusia's, Corey was the only one who worked with them. His two mares were now in foal.

A Frenchman, named Alberto Cuthbert, established a trading post up on the Musselshell River where it merged with the Missouri River. This was much closer than traveling all the way up to the Saskatchewan Province. Needing to set in supplies for the winter, Corey sent Panther up to the Cuthbert trading post to buy beans, potatoes and rice to store for the winter. He had Bear start digging out a root cellar and collect apples and blackberries from around the ranch. Corey selected a beautiful palomino stallion and four mares from his mustangs, then headed to the ARMS ranch. Until now they had survived on buffalo and elk meat, but it was uncertain if the herds would remain in the valleys during the winter months. Corey intended on trading the five horses for twenty five head of cattle. A start for a small herd meant only to provide them with food through the winters, and hides for blankets and outer garments.

As Corey rode into the compound of the ARMS Ranch, several ranch hands came rushing out to greet him. He had been very well liked by everyone on the ranch and they were very happy to see him. They wanted to know all about his new place. Mel came out and admonished him for staying away so long, and almost dragged him down off his horse to lead him inside. She was barking orders to everyone as she led him into the house.

"Billy, take his horses over to the corral and make sure they are fed and watered. Sky get some lemonade and bring it to the sitting room. Regina go set the table for lunch."

Once inside the house, Mel sat Corey down in the parlor, then ran upstairs to get Alejandra. Everyone with the exception of Corey himself knew Alejandra was in love with him. Even though she denied it, and got very upset when anyone brought up the subject. Mel knocked on her bedroom door, and without waiting for a reply, charged into Alejandra's bedroom. She was well aware of Corey's arrival and was applying fresh makeup.

Mel was getting impatient.

"For Christ sake, you couldn't look any lovelier, now get down there and welcome your guest."

Alejandra led the way down stairs. When she entered the parlor her knees buckled slightly at the sight of Corey. Gathering herself, she walked over to him and grabbed his hand, shaking it aggressively.

"Corey, it has been too long, you must tell me how your ranch is coming along?"

Corey was suddenly uncomfortable, although he didn't know why he should be uneasy, he has known Alejandra for the better part of a year now.

"Hello, Miss Strand, it is nice to see you again."

Alejandra was upset with his greeting.

"Miss Strand, do I look like your mother, Miss Strand indeed."

She was visibly upset that Corey would address her by her surname. She took it as a sign that Corey felt nothing for her, and that he could only see her as a fellow rancher. She had hoped his first visit back would be only to visit her, but it appeared by his demeanor that he was strictly here to conduct business.

Mel could see Alejandra's temper was getting the best of her, and before she exploded and said something she would regret, Mel interrupted.

"Corey, would you like a glass of lemonade?"

"Thank you Mel, I would, the ride over was warm and dry."

Mel grabbed Alejandra by the arm and dragged her into the kitchen. Once out of Corey's sight, Mel snapped at her.

"What is the matter with you. The first time you have seen him in almost seven months and you were just about to read him the riot act."

"He is being totally inconsiderate, *"Fine Miss Strand"*, like I was his mother or something."

"Alejandra, he doesn't know you are in love with him. How would you expect him to treat a woman of stature, if not politely and with manners?"

"I never said I was in love with him, what makes you think such a thing anyway?"

"Everyone but Corey knows you are in Love with him. You just refuse to admit it to anyone other than yourself. I'm not even sure your willing to admit it to yourself. He is here to trade mustangs for cattle. It must be important to him or he wouldn't have brought that beautiful palomino stallion for you. Now, I want you to take him out on the ranch and help him select the cattle. You can use Midnight as an excuse for the two of you to ride out together."

"Alright, but I don't know how long I can put up with his being non-attentive to me. Am I not beautiful enough for him? I thought he would show a little more emotion than to call me by my surname. After all, if it wasn't for me he would be lying dead out there in the meadow."

Mel's motherly talents were surely being tested today. But she refused to let these two give up on each other without a fight.

"It's obvious to the entire countryside that you two belong together, and if I have anything to do with it, you will be married. Alejandra, you need to be patient with him. Men like Corey don't just haul off and kiss a woman, or openly confess their love. Besides, how is he to know you are even interested in him? You haven't done anything to show him how you feel, or that you even care for him on a personal level. You have to do things that lets him know you are interested. When you're close to him, touch him tenderly, speak to him in a manner that will draw out his emotions and feelings. Right now he feels obligated to you for saving his life. You need to move him past that feeling of indebtedness before you can bring out his feelings of love for you."

Alejandra calmed down and understood what Mel was telling her.

"I never thought about him being so inexperienced. My only experience with men up to now has been with Trent Oswald back in Texas. He was always fawning all over me, brutally confessing his love whenever he saw me. He demanded my love rather than trying to earn my affection. To tell you the truth, every man I have ever met was the same. They never showed me any tenderness or respect, merely lust. I can see how Corey is different than all the others, I guess that is one of the reasons I love him so much. How can I let him know how I feel without telling him straight out and scarring him off?"

"While you are out riding the ranch together, ask him to stop so you can rest. Don't dismount right away, wait for him to assist you down from your saddle. Show him your feminine side, caress his arms as he releases you to the ground. keep your body close to his and let him draw in the scent of your perfume. It won't be long before he is calling you by your given name and expressing his devoted love for you."

"Isn't that just deceiving him?"

"No, it is taking him where he wants to go. If he doesn't love you, he will not continue to call on you outside of business. You will be able to tell by how he reacts to your touch. If he is interested he will respond positively. If he isn't interested, he will gently push you away, but in a fashion to let you know that he is here strictly to conduct business, and for no other reason."

They walked back into the dining room carrying the pitcher of lemonade and glasses. Alejandra spoke to Corey as Mel poured the lemonade.

"Tell me Corey, what brings you to the ARMS Ranch today?"

"I was hoping to trade horses for cattle. Until now, there has been plenty of buffalo and elk in the area to keep us fed. Although I am concerned that once the cold sets in, we won't be able to sustain ourselves by only hunting wild game. Having a few cattle to breed and slaughter for meat would help us survive the harsh winters."

"How many cows are you expecting in return for the five horses you have brought."

"The mustangs are some of my best horses. I was hoping to get twenty five head of cattle in return. I would like to have five longhorns and twenty of your highland cattle. I don't think the longhorns will be long for these harsh conditions. With at least two highland bulls I can sire the highland cattle for two or three years and end up with a large enough heard to more than support my ranch's need for beef. I will use the longhorns to feed us this winter and next, until the highland cattle have produced their first two seasons of offspring."

"I can see you have given this quite a bit of thought. Regina, have Octavio saddle Midnight up for me please. Midnight is the name I have given the mare you presented me. Did you ride Spirit over?"

"Yes."

"Then lets go see if we can select those cattle you want. But I must demand something more than the horses in return."

"I haven't brought but the five horses, and I don't have any cash for payment. What else can I give you?"

"You must agree to spend the evening and have dinner with us. You can return home with your cattle tomorrow. Grayson will have the cattle you select cut from the herd and placed in the holding pens. They will be ready for your trip back tomorrow."

"It would be my pleasure, and thank you very much for the invite. My cooking isn't much to talk about, and it will be nice to enjoy some of Mel's wonderful cooking again."

Mel was looking over at Alejandra and was sporting a huge smile. Letting her know she approved, and that she had handled herself well.

They had been riding for about a half hour, and Spirit was unsettled as Midnight was in season.

"Corey, why don't we stop and give the horses and ourselves a rest?"

"Good idea."

After dismounting, Corey walked over to Alejandra and lifted her down from the saddle. As her feet touched the ground, he seemed to linger, leaving his hands clasped around her waist, soaking up the aroma of Alejandra's perfume.

He was sweating again and blamed it on the heat. In reality, it was the sweet smell of Alejandra's perfume filling his senses, and the soft caress she gave him as he lowered her to the ground, that was making him sweat. Corey cleared his throat.

"Should we move out of the sun and sit in the shade?"

Alejandra could tell she had made a dent in his armor, he was no longer concerned about the cattle.

"Of course, maybe we could sit under that tree with the small shelf of grass jutting out. It would make a wonderful place to sit and stretch out our legs."

Corey apologized for letting his hands remain around her waist for an extended period of time.

"No need to apologize, I like the feel of your strong hands wrapped around me."

Corey was blushing, he hasn't had any real experience with women, and wasn't quite sure of what Alejandra's demeanor meant.

"Midnight is in season, I would like to unsaddle the horses and let Spirit breed with her. Not only will it keep the bloodline true, it will work out some of their frustrations, and I won't have to fight him so much on the ride back. Like I had to the entire ride out.

"Excellent idea, hurry, then come sit down beside me. We can talk about our desires and dreams while they get acquainted."

Spirit and Midnight frolicked in the pasture below, while Corey and Alejandra talked of how their lives had paralleled one another. Their hardships with ranching in Texas, their mothers dying when they were young and their fathers having been killed by ruthless men. They discussed their exploits traveling through the Unorganized Territory up to Montana.

Somewhere during the afternoon, Alejandra moved closer to Corey and laid her head on his shoulder. Spirit and Midnight had finished mating and were feeding close by their blanket. Corey shifted his position as if he was going to stand up, Alejandra was about to state her dissatisfaction with his getting up to leave. Then Corey wrapped his arms around her and pulled her close to him for a kiss. Alejandra turned her body to meet his and responded with a deep kiss of her own. She pressed her mouth to his with all the tenderness she could muster. Holding the kiss for a much longer period than one might give as a response of friendship.

Corey slowly released his hold on her and stood up. As much as he wanted to, Corey didn't know how to express his feeling out loud. He extended a hand down for Alejandra's, she gave it to him freely as he pulled her to her feet only inches from him. The smell of her perfume was once again filling his nostrils, his head was swimming with confusion.

"I am sorry Alejandra, I don't know what came over me. Please forgive me for being so forward, but my feelings for you go far beyond that of friendship."

"*Corey Kittridge*, don't you dare apologize for kissing me and letting your feelings be known. I have been waiting for you to notice me for nearly a year now. And all I have gotten was, "**Miss this**" and "**Miss that**". Now that you have taken notice and confessed your feelings for me, you want to apologize. I'll not have you treat me in that manner."

Alejandra wrapped her arms around his neck, pulled him close and kissed him hard and long. When she released him, he was overwhelmed by her actions. Not knowing what to say, or do, he wrapped his arms around her midriff and pulled her close as he returned her kiss.

He gave her one last quick peck on the cheek before releasing her. Without saying another word he gathered the horses. Alejandra was watching him skillfully saddle the horses, smiling the whole time. There was no doubt in her mind, Corey loves her, even if he is to bashful or inexperienced to know how to say the words out loud.

After cutting out the cattle he wanted, Corey moved them away from the main herd and left them grazing one draw over from the main herd. They rode back to the house, mostly in silence, however, their expressions were filled with smiles and you could see the pride on their faces. What little talk there was, revolved around the cattle Corey had selected. After dinner Corey stood and said good night, then started to make his way to the bunkhouse, Mel realized where he was going and yelled out at him.

"Where do you think you're headed?"

"To the bunkhouse to get some sleep in preparation for tomorrow. It has been a long day, what with the ride over and then riding the range to select my cattle. Tomorrow will be another long day herding twenty five cattle through the pass all alone."

"You will do no such thing."

Mel had already been filled in by Alejandra of the day's events.

"Sky will bunk with Regina tonight, so you can stay in her room. You are no longer a ranch hand here, and therefore will not be treated as one."

"That doesn't seem fair to Sky. I'll be fine down at the bunkhouse."

"I am not going to say it again. Sky's room is the second room on the right as you get to the top of the stairs. Straight across from Alejandra's room. I'll wake you for breakfast."

Corey had a restless night, continually reliving the afternoon's activities with Alejandra in his mind. Still savoring the sweet smell of her perfume. He wasn't sure if her affections for him were real, or if she was merely toying with him. After all, she was a successful rancher, what did he have to offer other than a fledgling horse ranch.

Alejandra on the other hand, slept better than she had over the past five years. She had no doubt that the affection shown by Corey was heart felt. She awoke early wanting to beat Corey downstairs. It was not to be though, Corey was awake well before sunrise due to his restlessness, and had already been out to the stables and saddled his horse.

As he sat down for breakfast, all the women, with the exception of Alejandra, were giggling. Corey blushed, realizing Alejandra had probably told them of yesterday's adventure. Finished with breakfast, he thanked Mel for the great meal and said his goodbyes. He walked out to the corral, Spirit was anxious and ready to hit the trail. As Corey started to open the gate, Alejandra placed her hands on his shoulders. He turned, and with everyone watching wrapped his arms around her, gently hugging her while he bent his head over and kissed her goodbye. He gathered his cattle from the holding pen and headed them toward the pass.

Chapter 8

The ride back took much longer than he had expected. Herding the cattle by himself through the forest and hills was a lot harder than moving a herd over open prairies and the desert. Even though there was only twenty five head. It was dusk before he got them back to his ranch and into the corral.

Panther returned from the trading post with the supplies, and Bear had a good beginning on the root cellar. For the next two days, all three of them worked on the root cellar. It was important that they got it finished to store the meat, fruits and vegetables.

After completing the root cellar, they all worked in the fields, cutting fresh grass to feed the cattle during the worst of the winter. It helped that the Highland cattle were very hearty animals with long hair and thick coats. They were from Scotland and bred for surviving such harsh winters. They would feed on scrub bushes and weeds more than the American breeds, and would dig through the deep snow for forage.

By the time they had finished cutting the last of the winter hay and storing it under the sheds to keep it dry, the temperatures had started to drop significantly. They moved the cattle into a boxed canyon so they could get used to their new boundaries. While it wasn't a true box canyon as the one the horses were in, the pastures were surrounded by mountain ridges and the Bighorn River. It was enough to keep them from leaving the comfort of the lush pasture and water.

Corey wanted to ride over and visit Alejandra before snow filled the pass. This time he took Panther and Bear along with him. With the exception of Regina and Jason, none of the ARMS ranch hands or women had ever been introduced to them. Panther and Bear's English was much improved, which helped significantly in meeting everyone for the first time. After introductions, everyone sat around a camp fire to enjoy the barbecued beef.

Corey and Alejandra snuck off behind the barn, hugging and kissing each other as if they had been apart for a lifetime. Corey confessed his disappointment with having not been able to see her over the length of the summer. Although the distance between their ranches wasn't that far, he impressed upon her how important it was to get his ranch in working order. It was imperative he get it set up and provisioned to make it through the first winter. Only then could he enjoy the luxury of relaxing. Alejandra knew all to well what Corey was saying was true. She expressed her understanding and pressed her lips against his once again.

Corey didn't want to let her go, but knew if they didn't return soon the others would be looking for them. As they stepped around the corner of the barn everyone started giggling. Corey blushed as Alejandra joined in on the laughter. Corey and Alejandra went on a ride later in the afternoon. They discussed their plans for the future mostly, but occasionally interrupted the talk to share their affection for one another.

Alejandra had given marriage serious thought, and thought Corey felt as she did about them getting married.

"Corey, why do you need your own ranch? Why don't you come live on the ARMS Ranch so we can be together always?"

He knew no matter what he said at this point, other than he would move onto the ARMS Ranch, Alejandra was going to be disappointed.

"I can't Alejandra..."

Corey was instantly interrupted, as soon as Alejandra heard the word "can't", with Corey's somber tone, she started sobbing.

"Can't, you mean won't. Your horses mean more to you than I do."

"That's not true Alejandra. The horses have nothing to do with it, I just don't want people saying my only interest in you is for your ranch, and not because I love you. I have to establish myself first. Besides, we haven't even had a formal courtship."

"I don't care what other people may or may not think. I love you, and I want to be with you."

"And I love you too, but I don't want my wife thought of negatively because of me. You are one of the most powerful rancher's in the area, not to mention the most beautiful. I want everyone to know we married for love, and not for the power you wield, or the wealth associated with your ranch. If you have any respect for me at all, you'll let me court you properly, and wait until I have the means to support you before we get married. Whether you need my support or not."

"I think you are being too old fashioned, but I'll wait. Don't you stay away from me so long this time, or I may just find someone else who will marry me."

They both laughed, then hugged each other tight. Alejandra found it peculiar that Corey loved her, but wouldn't marry her because of her wealth. Trent Oswald always wielded his wealth as a sword, demanding she marry him, without once ever telling her he loved her.

Mel made chicken fried steak, mashed potatoes and fried okra for dinner. They all ate outside while enjoying the sunset and talking. After dinner, Corey, Panther and Bear mounted up and headed back to the Kittridge Ranch. It was a long ride for Corey, he was wondering if he had made a mistake by not accepting Alejandra's offer to move onto the ARMS Ranch and marry her.

While he was sulking on the trail, considering whether or not he had made a mistake. Mel was assuring Alejandra that having a formal courtship was the proper way to proceed. That Corey needed to establish himself and his ranch so he would feel worthy of her love. That she should support him in that desire.

Corey made a point of riding over to see Alejandra at least once a week for the next month and a half. It was November when the first snows fell. Corey commented to Alejandra that the snows seemed heavier than normal for this time of the year. She just chalked it up to Corey being new to the area, and not used to snow this early in the season, especially having lived in Texas all his life.

It was Saturday night and Corey was preparing to ride over to Alejandra's in the morning. He promised to take her to the new church built in the town of River Bend. That night three feet of snow fell. Corey had to climb out the window of his house to clear the snow away from in front of the door so he could open it. Then he went to the bunkhouse and dug out Panther and Bear.

"I don't think you can make it over to Miss Strand's today boss."

"No Panther, the pass will have drift snow too deep to cross. It looks like we may be snowed in for awhile. I want you and Bear to move into the main house. It will be easier to heat and cook for the three of us there, instead of trying to heat the bunkhouse at the same time. Besides, if the winter is as bad as I think it is going to be, we will have to use our wood sparingly to make it last all winter."

Corey was wishing he had not put off building the front porch on the house.

Alejandra felt the chill of the morning when she awoke. Lying under the down comforter she was smiling at the thought of Corey coming over to take her to church. If she was lucky, he would forget this nonsense about courting and just ask her to marry her today. They could be married while at church.

She was quickly brought back to reality when Sky started beating on her door, yelling for her to come downstairs. Alejandra jumped up out of bed, dressing quickly as she wondered what could be the problem. When she reached the bottom of the stairs, the other three women were pressed together looking out the front door.

"What is it, what's wrong?"

Mel turned around and looked at her with a saddened look on her face. Normally the sight of snow was a good thing, and they enjoyed it, but Mel knew how much Alejandra was looking forward to Corey taking her to church. That was not going to happen today. It was certain no one could travel through the pass with this much snow.

Alejandra didn't want to show her disappointment, and before anyone could say anything else, she started issuing orders. Regina, make sure the men can get out of the bunkhouse. Sky, help Grayson break up the ice in the water troughs so the horses can drink. Mel, you best get breakfast started, they'll be hungry after working in the cold. I'll help Rusty and Devon fork hay down from the loft.

The temperature had dropped well below freezing, making work in the elements difficult and extremely slow. It wasn't until early afternoon before they finished their tasks of ensuring both the ranch hands and animals would be safe from the weather. Everyone sat in silence as they ate a hot meal. Not only were they exhausted, they knew how disappointed Alejandra was about Corey not being unable to take her to church. Whether she admitted it or not.

For the next two weeks the weather cooperated and they got nothing more than a few flurries. However, the temperatures remained very low, so the snow that had fallen remained on the ground. During the down time Bear showed Corey how to make snow shoes. He couldn't believe the difference the snow shoes made in getting around.

They spent most of their days working close to the house. Shoring up the roofs and making sure the horses had access to water. After a week had passed, they ventured out to the pastures to check on the cattle and horses. They rigged a light weight sled and using the draft horses, pulled bales of hay out to the pasture.

The cattle were in surprisingly good shape. The highland cattle proved to be good scavengers as advertised. None had died from the extreme cold. However, the four remaining longhorns were showing signs of weakness. Under normal conditions they might not have been affected, but the extreme cold this early on without the protection of thick hair and hides like the highland cattle, the weather took it's toll on them.

"Panther, throw a loop over one of the longhorns and take him to the barn, the other three should follow you back."

As soon as Corey had brought them back from the ARMS Ranch, they butchered one of the longhorns for its beef and hide. They smoked and salted most of the meat and stored it in the root cellar. Although they made sure to cut several steaks for frying. Keeping the longhorns in the barn area could ensure they're survival should the weather keep them from getting out to the pastures.

Panther, on his own initiative, had bought five laying hens and a rooster, when he purchased the supplies Corey had sent him to get at Cuthbert's trading post. The barn made a natural roost and offered them plenty of protection from the elements and predators. Having eggs to eat proved to make a big difference in their diet, not to mention their dispositions.

For the next few weeks they moved snow out of the ranch yard using the sled and draft horses. When not doing that, they continued to work on the buildings, chinking the logs to weather proof the walls and keep the inside dry and warm.

Corey decided it was time to make a trip over to the ARMS Ranch. Naturally he was most interested in seeing Alejandra, but he was concerned for all of them and their well being. The snow was still to deep for a horse to travel through, so he and Bear strapped on their snowshoes and headed out at first light. Panther was left behind to care for the livestock, and to keep the ice broken up in the water troughs.

Travel was slow having to walk in the snow and cold. Not only because of the elements, but also because of their heavy clothing that restricted their movements. They were a day and a half out when they met Sky, who was out looking for deer or elk. Her father had taught her how to track and hunt as good as any mountain man.

While sitting around a small fire talking about horses, Corey's plans for the ranch and eating jerky, they heard the crunch of the snow directly below them. Quickly Sky and Bear vanished back into the trees. It was obvious the sound was made by a man and not an animal. Corey remained at the fire as if nothing was wrong. He was warming his hands when the two Sioux warriors stepped out of the trees and walked up behind him. Corey stood up and walked around the fire so he was facing them.

Corey motioned for the two warriors to sit at the fire. Then, reaching into his pocket he pulled out a couple pieces of jerky and offered it to them. It was obvious they didn't understand what he was saying, and he didn't speak enough Sioux to make them understand

Taking a chance, Corey decided to speak in Crow, hoping they might understand him better. The Sioux immediately backed up, keeping a close eye on him while they notched their bows. The Crow and Sioux were natural enemies, and this white man was speaking their tongue. They were scared that the white man was trying to lure them into a trap, and to kill them while their guard was down. The Sioux started yelling at him at the same time they were drawing back the strings on their bows. Corey had never bothered to remove the leather thong holding down the hammer on his pistol. Not that it would have made a difference, his pistol was hidden well under his coat, making it impossible to get to quickly enough anyway.

Just as the Sioux were about to let loose their arrows, Sky spoke out from behind a tree. One of the Sioux turned his attention to Sky, while the other kept Corey covered. The voice told them to stop and lower their weapons, that they were with friends. Sky stepped out from behind the tree to reassure them it wasn't a trick. The Sioux were still unaware of Bear, who remained hidden, holding aim with his rifle. The only reason he hadn't shot, was that he was afraid he couldn't kill them both before one of them put an arrow into Corey.

Even though her father was a white man, she retained many of the Sioux features she inherited from her mother, and spoke Sioux fluently. Continuing to speak to them in their own language she tried to calm them down so no one would have to die.

"We are friends. We mean you no harm."

It was the larger of the two braves that spoke.

"What is your name, and how is it you speak our language?"

"My name is Skah, daughter of Willie Pike, the Mountain Man, and Little Bear, daughter of White Buffalo."

Both men had heard of the mountain man Willie Pike who had saved Chief White Buffalo. The story goes, that Pike saved White Buffalo from a grizzly bear. That he put his own life in danger by using only his hunting knife to kill the bear, because he couldn't get a shot off without hitting White Buffalo. Chief White Buffalo has since passed away.

"Is this man keeping you prisoner?"

"No, he is my friend. What brings you so far north from your lands?"

"Food, the buffalo have left the hills and went down to the low lands where the white man and Cheyenne live. Food is scarce and we have to travel farther out each day to find the deer and elk. This man you call your friend, he is a friend to the Crow. He catches horses for them to replenish their herds. We thought we killed him when we tried to steal his horses last year."

"You put three arrows into him, but he did not die. He owns the Kittridge Ranch, and I am part owner of the ARSM Ranch. Miss Strand saved him and his horses from you. We do not seek any trouble. We want to be friends with the Sioux and live in peace."

"Since he speaks and catches horses for the Crow, does he fight with them too?"

Sky knew anything she said now may or may not be believed. She turned and pointed to Corey, then spoke to him using the Crow's language. She did this so the Sioux would understand the questions she asked of Corey, and his responses.

"Corey, I am going to ask you some questions, you should give your answers using the Crow's tongue. Do you hate the Sioux?"

"No, I wish to be their friends and live in peace along side them."

"Do you have a desire to fight or kill the Sioux?"

"No, I have no desire to harm any of the Sioux people, or any other tribe for that matter. I am a horseman and wish only to live in peace with all Indian tribes. I will not take up arms with any one tribe against another, unless I am forced to do so in the defense of my life, or my friends lives."

The Sioux un-notched their arrows and lowered their bows.

"We will spread the word to our people. The Kittridge and ARMS ranches will be considered friends of the Sioux until proven otherwise. My name is Shadow Hawk, Chief of all Sioux hunters, this is Stalking Cougar."

Corey spoke to Bear and asked him to step out with his arms and rifle raised high. Bear did as Corey asked, yet as a Crow he was very untrusting. He kept his finger on the trigger for a quick shot if needed. Corey could see the displeased look on Shadow Hawk's face when he called Bear out from behind the trees. Even more so when he realized Bear was a Crow.

"Chief, this is Bear, he and another Crow named Panther, work for me and live on my ranch. They are also friends and have no desire to harm you or your people. Bear could have killed you just now had he wished, but he didn't. He and Panther only wish to live in peace, as I do."

Shadow Hawk could feel Corey's honesty, and tell he was speaking the truth. Bear could have killed him and Stalking Cougar easily had he wanted, but he didn't.

"I will let it be known that Bear and Panther are also friends to the Sioux people."

Still speaking in Crow, since everyone understood that language, he gave instructions to Bear.

"Bear, take Shadow Hawk and Stalking Cougar back to the ranch. Give them one of our longhorns to help feed their people. I will make arrangements with the Arms Ranch for more longhorns . Shadow Hawk, come back to my ranch in one moon, and I will have more cattle for you and your people. Bring trade goods to swap for the cattle."

Corey knew it was important that the Sioux give him something in exchange for the cattle. To not require something in trade, the Sioux would have been shamed if the cattle were offered as a gift, and nothing was required as payment.

Each placed one hand on top the other's shoulder, and shook with the other, at that moment Corey and Shadow Hawk became friends. Bear led the Sioux warriors back to the Kittridge Ranch. Corey continued on to the ARMS Ranch with Sky.

Chapter 9

Bear instructed Shadow Hawk and his warrior to stay hidden in the trees until he could inform Panther about the agreement. Panther was beside himself. Not only did he have to befriend the Sioux, but they also had to give up one of their longhorns to feed them. However, this is what Corey wished of him, and he liked living on the Kittridge Ranch. Life was far better here than trying to survive in a teepee.

Not wanting to disappoint Corey, Panther placed his rifle against the wall and stepped outside with his hands high in the air to show he was unarmed. Shadow Hawk and his companion walked down to greet him. As they talked and got better acquainted, Bear went to the barn to retrieve one of the longhorns. He returned with the bull to find the other three men laughing. Panther reached out and took the lead rope from Bear and handed it to Shadow Hawk. Smiling, Shadow Hawk accepted the bull and left waiving goodbye.

Including the numerous stops to rest, it took Corey the better part of three days to cover the fifteen miles between the two ranches. A trek that normally only took 3 to 4 hours on horseback. Alejandra couldn't believe her eyes as she stared out the front window. Sky and Corey were walking into the ranch yard.

Unconcerned about the cold, she ran outside without a coat and jumped into Corey's arms, kissing him several times before saying hello. Sky was watching with delight. She and Mel were still without a lover or male companionship, but they both remained hopeful. Alejandra had Corey and Regina was with Jason.

Corey swept Alejandra up in his arms and carried her back into the house. He was having trouble catching his breath and unable to talk with Alejandra smothering him in kisses. When they entered the Parlor, Mel emerged from the kitchen with hot coffee and biscuits for Corey and Sky. Corey told the story of meeting Sky, and their encounter with Shadow Hawk and Stalking Cougar.

"If it had not been for Sky, I would be lying dead in the snow with a Sioux arrow sticking out of my chest. Bear would have killed them, but not before they killed me."

Alejandra was very thankful Corey was alive, and agreed to provide him with twelve longhorns to take back with him for trading with the Sioux. If true, and the ranch was now safe from attack by the Sioux, life was about to get a lot easier in the Montana wilderness.

Sky offered to bunk with Mel and give Corey her room. He usually bunked in Regina's room, but Sky knew Jason was prone to visiting Regina at night now. Since Jason was out working the pastures, he wouldn't know Corey was visiting, and Regina didn't want Jason being surprised when he found another man in her bed.

Alejandra instructed Rusty to ride out with Devon and round up a dozen longhorns, six of the weakest and six strong ones. If the weak ones weren't butchered for food soon, they would die during the harsh winter anyway and will have been of no use to anyone. If they could help bring peace with the Sioux, then all the better.

Corey and Alejandra cozied up in front of the fireplace, and talked about how his ranch was coming along. Corey was finally starting to thaw out from the cold that had buried deep into his bones. It was late and Mel declared it was time for bed. Corey entered Sky's bedroom and stripped out of his clothes down to his underwear.

Corey was just slipping into a restful sleep when he heard the hallway floor creak, followed by the bedroom door opening.

"Sky, what is it, did you forget something?"

"I didn't forget anything sweetheart, I just didn't want to be alone tonight."

Corey was shocked, it was Alejandra.

"Alejandra, what are you doing in here?"

She didn't answer as she crossed the room, raised the blanket, and slipped in beside Corey.

After a few tender kisses, Alejandra whispered into his ear.

"Go to sleep darling, you have a hard couple of days ahead of you."

Wrapped in each others arms they fell asleep, each enjoying the warmth of the other. Corey was awake before the sun rose. He watched Alejandra as she slept in the crease of his shoulder. She was still wearing her full length white cotton nightgown. He turned his head and kissed her softly on the forehead. He was thankful Alejandra had only wanted to be close to him, and did not desire to make love that night. It was clear he desired her, but he didn't want to soil her reputation for one night's weakness.

Alejandra woke up from the pressure of the kiss, and rolled over to hug him tight. She quickly slipped out from underneath the covers and returned to her own bedroom. As she reached the bedroom door, she thanked Corey for being a gentleman, and respecting her enough not to take advantage of the situation. While she didn't say it to him, she knew she would not have resisted any advance he might have made to make love to her.

Not more than fifteen minutes later Mel came knocking on the bedroom doors.

"Wake up everyone, breakfast is being served. Let's go kids, the chores aren't going to get done by themselves."

She opened Alejandra's bedroom door and peaked in with a big grin on her face.

"Just checking, did you enjoy yourself last night?"

She doesn't know how, but Alejandra was certain Mel knew she spent the night with Corey. At breakfast Alejandra instructed Grayson to have Jason and Devon help Corey get the longhorns through the pass and back to his ranch. Also to pass the word of their new peace accord with the Sioux. If they encounter any Sioux, they are not to engage them in battle.

Two days later they arrived at the Kittridge Ranch with all twelve longhorns. Jason and Devon stayed overnight in the bunkhouse, and after breakfast headed back home. They were better than halfway back when they crossed paths with a Sioux hunting party. Shadow Hawk was one of them, but this trip he had a member of the tribe that spoke English.

Jason reminded Devon that they were not to start any trouble and to keep his hands away from his guns. After several minutes of talking, Shadow Hawk learned the two men worked on the ARMS Ranch. They parted friends and went on about their own ways. Devon expressed his surprise to Jason, saying he wouldn't have believed it if he hadn't been a part of it and seen it with his own eyes. The Sioux, now friends of the Kittridge and ARMS Ranch.

Shadow Hawk was actually pleased by the friendly encounter between them and the two men of the ARMS Ranch. Before Corey had befriended the Sioux, in just about that same location, the Sioux and the men of the ARMS Ranch would have fought to the death. He thought how unfortunate it was that the miners and army could not accept the Sioux as equals, or trusted to hold a peace like the men and women of the Kittridge and ARMS ranches.

It's been two days since Shadow Hawk and his hunting party crossed paths with the Jason and Devon, and they still had not sighted any deer or elk. He decided to head back to the encampment by way of the Kittridge Ranch. With any luck they would be successful in their hunt for food before reaching the ranch.

Three days had passed before they walked up to the Kittridge Ranch, and still they not seen or killed any game to feed their tribe. Corey learned a few more words and phrases in Sioux, so he greeted Shadow Hawk in his own tongue. Then he switched back to speaking Crow to speed up the conversation. Shadow Hawk had been confident they would be successful on the hunt, therefore, he had brought no furs or anything to trade for cattle.

Corey expressed his sorrow for Shadow Hawk's unsuccessful hunt. The Sioux, like everyone else needed meat to survive the winter. With the number of newcomers traveling through the area, and the early start to winter, game has become scarce. They had been driven down to the lower lands by the cold winter, and over hunted to meet the needs of the miners and pioneers.

Corey gave Shadow Hawk the six weakest longhorns, telling him he could bring the trade goods back later. Even though the longhorns were weak from the cold, and would not survive the winter, they still carried a lot of beef. Once again this white man had shown kindness to the Sioux, asking nothing in return but a promise. Shadow Hawk exclaimed that the entire Lakota nation would be made aware of his generosity and friendship. From this day forward, the entire Lakota Nation was to consider Corey Kittridge a brother.

Panther and Bear could not believe their ears. In the Sioux's entire history there hasn't been more than two other white men ever considered a brother. One was Sky's father, Willie Pike, who saved their Chief White Buffalo, and the other was a buffalo hunter named William.

It didn't take long for the kindness Corey displayed toward the Sioux tribe to spread throughout the Lakota and Crow nations. Neither tribe was happy he had befriended the other, but both understood he would not take up arms against either tribe on behalf of the other. Corey continued to catch horses for the Crow and provide beef to the Sioux. The Crow still received their beef from the ARMS Ranch.

The Sioux were now restricting their hunting to the south end of the Bighorn Basin, where there was still some elk and buffalo. Even so they traded for the remaining six longhorns Corey had gotten from Alejandra. The Sioux gave Corey buffalo hides and beaver furs in return for the cattle. The hides and furs were valued at three times the cost of the cattle, but the lives the cattle saved were worth far more than any furs to the Sioux.

Corey used a quarter of the furs to trade for supplies at Cuthbert's trading post. He kept the hides to make blankets and coats. Finally he sold the remaining furs to Cuthbert. He gave the cash he received from Cuthbert for the remaining furs to Alejandra. She only accepted an amount equal to what the cattle were worth, and handed the rest back to Corey.

"Alejandra, the cash you gave me back is too much."

"You deserve it Corey, if for nothing else for the peace you brokered between us and the Sioux. Besides, I know you are in need of cash. I have no reason to cheat you and charge you more than the going price."

Corey accepted the cash back without any further argument. The rest of the winter passed without incident. Although cold, and with a greater than normal amount of snow, the ranches made it through the winter without to much hardship.

Corey managed to get over and see Alejandra on three more occasions during the last two and a half months. After the first big thaw he wasn't surprised to see Alejandra, Regina, Sky, Jason, and a couple other ranch hands ride up to his house. Jason and Regina helped Bear put together a big plate of sandwiches while Corey started a fresh pot of coffee.

"Sorry, we don't have any tea or lemonade, just coffee." Then he laughed and said, "Maybe you should have brought Mel along."

Alejandra smiled, then kissed him on the cheek.

"That's okay cowboy, coffee will do just fine."

Sitting around the outdoor table, Sky shocked everyone with her confession that she has been seeing Shadow Hawk. Even Alejandra was taken by surprise.

"Sky, why didn't you say anything?"

"I wasn't sure how you would feel about me dating someone that has been your enemy for the better part of five years. Besides, his tribe is still at war with the white man and the Crow. The Sioux still have concerns about us being friends with the Crow, it wouldn't take much to break the peace."

"It is alright, we will support your relationship with Shadow Hawk. You are welcome to bring him to the ranch anytime you wish. You can teach me and Corey to speak the Sioux language so we can make him feel more comfortable when he is around us. It will also be beneficial to us when you or Shadow Hawk are not around, and we should encounter any other Sioux Indians."

Sky was overjoyed with the reaction and support shown by everyone.

"Thank you so very much, I will let him know he is accepted and welcome to visit the ranch."

Chapter 10

The following Sunday, Corey took Alejandra to church in River Bend as he had promised.

Hugo Maddox and his son Jacob were standing outside the church, waiting for the last of the stragglers to enter the church. He liked to think when he entered the church, it was a signal for the Preacher to begin the services. In reality, the Preacher merely waited to close the door until after all his parishioners had entered, and were seated before starting the services. It had nothing to do with Maddox himself, it was simply that Maddox was usually the last one to enter the church for services.

As Corey and Alejandra walked up the path, Hugo Maddox stepped out in front of them and introduced himself and his son to Corey, then re-acquainted himself with Alejandra.

"Miss Strand", Hugo said as he tipped his hat. "It is a pleasure to see you again. I hope your ranch survived the rough winter without too much difficulty."

"Good morning Mr. Maddox, thank you for your concern. We did just fine. We lost very few head of cattle, and the calf crop is in good condition. How about yourself, any problems?"

"We did fine also, though some of the smaller ranchers didn't fair so well. Grant and Meeker sold out to me and left for Oregon. How about you Mr. Kittridge, are you in the cattle business?"

"No, I am a horse breeder, although I worked on a cattle ranch most of my life."

"Horses, huh. Doesn't seem like there is much call for a horse breeder in this area. What we don't catch ourselves, we buy from the Crow. You do know the Crow are considered the best horse people around."

"Yes, I do, and I don't intend to compete against them. Who knows though, maybe some day even you will find my services of value."

"I wouldn't hold my breath, ain't nothing a Texas refugee could offer me. I was breaking horses when you were still in diapers."

"I'll remember you said that."

Corey had never mentioned being from Texas, and Alejandra hadn't mentioned speaking with Maddox during the winter.

"By the way, how is it you know I am from Texas?"

Maddox stood frozen for a second. He had made a mistake saying that, and he couldn't let on that he took on a new partner from Texas, Forest Vance.

"Your accent, all you Texan's have that unmistakable draw. Come on Jacob let's move inside and take our seats."

Corey didn't like Maddox's attitude, or rude remarks. He was certain, had it not been for Alejandra being at his side, that Maddox would have been more hostile towards him.

"Alejandra, does Maddox know you are from Texas, or has he said anything to you about my being from Texas?"

"Now that you mention it, he specifically asked where I hailed from when we first met. He guessed I was from Louisiana, and when I said west Texas, he said he never would have guessed. He never inquired of me as to where you lived prior to your coming to the Bighorn Basin."

"How long has he been ranching in the territory?"

"He arrived two years after I did. He brought in a large herd and bought the biggest ranch in the area with cash. Mr. Aaron, the previous owner, was getting on in age, and was tired of fighting the Indians and the elements, so he sold out. Needless to say, Maddox bought the ranch at a bargain price since there were no other serious buyers. Not long after being here he started running roughshod over the small ranchers. If he had his way, he would be the only rancher north of the Bozeman Trail. I don't know if you noticed it or not, but half the businesses in town have his name over the door. Not to mention he has the largest mining operation in the area."

"I don't like him, he and his son Jacob remind me of the Vance's back in Texas."

Corey had no idea how ironic that statement was, what with Forest Vance being an equal partner of the Maddox ranch.

"Don't let him worry you sweetheart. It was probably nothing more than an offhanded comment. More than likely he just said that because there are a lot of Texans moving north. Let's get inside so we can find a seat and not have to stand up in the back."

The sermon was full of fire and brimstone. The Preacher railed of the lord's judgment against those who drink and fornicate in the saloons. Alejandra was oblivious to it all, she was day dreaming of standing before the pulpit in a beautiful white flowing gown as she and Corey traded wedding vows.

All the way home Alejandra held onto Corey's arm, as he muddled over the disrespect Maddox showed towards him. Corey decided it was time to drift back toward Texas and find out what, if anything, was posted with regard to his being wanted for murder. Also he needed to find out if there was a bounty being offered.

Upon arriving back at the Ranch, Rusty, who had been assigned the duties of horse wrangler upon Corey's departure, was leaning against the corral. Stepping forward as they approached, he grabbed hold of the trace reins and held the horse as Corey lifted Alejandra down from the buckboard.

"Good evening Mr. Kittridge, Ms. Strand, I'll take care of the buggy, ya'll go on inside."

Alejandra was more than capable of stepping down from the buggy without assistance, but she loved having Corey's hands wrapped around her waist.

"Thank you Rusty, after you put the buggy away we won't need you anymore tonight."

Corey seconded her comments. He had no intentions of leaving Alejandra before morning.

"Alright ma'am, but if your new man doesn't measure up, I'll be in the bunkhouse."

Everyone within ear shot herd Rusty's joke and broke out in laughter, including Alejandra and Corey.

Corey stayed in the guest room on the first floor. This was where he slept now when staying overnight. That didn't keep Alejandra from visiting him during the night, where they would fall asleep holding each other in their arms.

Corey got an early start back to his own ranch. Alejandra was disappointed with his early departure.

She chalked it up to his having been away for two days, and needing to get back and tend to chores. She had no idea he was preparing to ride south to clear his name of murder.

The truth was, Corey had planned to stay with Alejandra a few days and court her, and then ask her to marry him. It was Maddox's comments that changed his mind. He had to know what Maddox knew about him, and if he was in danger of being exposed, or worse, being hunted. Either way, he couldn't risk putting Alejandra in danger as a result of his troubles with Vance and the law. He had to clear his name before he could even consider asking Alejandra to be his bride.

Corey spent the day preparing to leave for an extended period of time. He went through all the things Panther and Bear needed to do around the ranch during his absence. With one final thing to do, he asked Panther to prepare a pack with supplies for a month.

As Panther prepared the pack, Corey stepped inside the house and wrote out his will. It left the ranch to Panther and Bear as equal partners. He left his Andalusian horses to Alejandra. He wrote a provision that ensured Panther and Bear would continue to provide beef to Shadow Hawk and the Sioux tribe in times of famine. He made one last provision. His will was not to be made public, to anyone, especially Alejandra, until his death was confirmed.

Corey tossed and turned all night thinking of how Maddox might have learned of his troubles in Texas. Unable to sleep, he headed to the barn well before sunup to load the pack mule, and get Spirit ready to travel. He was surprised to see a lantern lit in the barn as he stepped out of the house. When he entered the barn, he saw Panther saddling his horse, he had already loaded up the mule. Panther turned and faced Corey as he entered the barn.

"I couldn't sleep either boss. So I done readied your horse and mule for you."

"Thanks Panther, that was very kind of you. I have come to consider you and Bear to be really good friends, not just ranch hands."

"Boss, you take care of yourself and come back to us. We would much rather be working with you, than own the ranch."

"Panther, get in touch with Rusty, the new horse wrangler on the ARMS Ranch. Tell him to ride into River Bend once a week and look for a message from me. I will sign it Matthew. If you need to get a message to me, give it to him, he will know how to get in touch with me."

Corey headed west as the sun peeked over the horizon. He had been unaware of the man that followed him from Alejandra's and watched him from atop the hill the day before.

Chapter 11

After church, Maddox returned to his ranch and informed Vance of his conversation with Kittridge. He told Vance about mistakenly saying he didn't need advice from a refugee out of Texas. Vance was visibly upset by this news. Kittridge may now be on notice someone is tracking him. At the same time, he was pleased to find out Corey was still in the area.

He learned of Kittridge's whereabouts by a miner passing through Santa Fe on his way to Los Angeles. But it was still speculation as to whether it was Kittridge or not, the miner was only repeating a story he had heard while mining up at River Bend. It was being said that a Texas gunfighter was saved from a Sioux war party by the Strand woman. The miner hadn't actually seen Kittridge.

A month after Corey's escape, the regional magistrate arrived in Eagle Creek. The local residents and ranchers all signed a petition to have Corey's arrest warrant for murder overturned. The magistrate conducted an investigation, and based upon the findings, he vacated the warrant, dismissing all charges against Corey Kittridge. The investigation proved the Vance brothers had been rustling cattle and horses to increase their own herds, then sold the rebranded stock to the Army. It was also determined the Commanding Officer of Fort Arbuckle was guilty of conspiring with the Vance brothers to purchase stolen stock, and for taking bribes. He was relieved of his command and dishonorably discharged.

Vance hated Kittridge for shooting his brother. Even though Tyrone was a ruthless killer, and Forest didn't agree with his methods, he was still kin. Now Kittridge has been exonerated of all charges, and Vance himself was forced to flee Texas. He was only one step ahead of the hangman's noose for cattle rustling.

Maddox was the story of Kittridge killing Tyrone Vance by Forest Vance. Although, Forest made it sound like Kittridge shot his brother in cold blood. Not giving him a chance to defend himself.   Maddox needed money to expand his mining operations, and Vance showed up at the right time with plenty of cash.

Vance promised Maddox the cash he needed to continue his mining operation, blinding Maddox to all else. He failed to take even the simplest of precautions and wire a telegram to the Eagle Creek sheriff to verify Vance's story. Had he done so, he would have known there was an active warrant out on Vance for rustling, and that Kittridge was innocent of any wrongdoing.

Hearing Maddox confess to putting Kittridge on notice, Vance immediately sent his hired gun, Chad Bentley, to the Strand Woman's ranch. Bentley had been one of Tyrone's top gun hands and Forest paid him well to stick by his side. He was instructed not to kill Kittridge, only to follow him and find out where he was holding up, then report back.

Bentley camped out in the hills above the ARMS Ranch where he could watch the entire compound without being noticed. When it was obvious Kittridge was going to spend the night, he rolled out his bed roll and went to sleep himself. By the time he awakened, Kittridge's horse was already saddled and he was mounting up to leave. Bentley had merely loosened the cinch on his saddle the night before, instead of removing the saddle from his horse. He wanted his horse saddled in case he had to move fast. So after tightening the cinch, he saddled up and followed Kittridge.

Bentley followed from a safe distance to ensure he wouldn't be seen in case Kittridge decided to check his back trail. At the same time Corey was entering the ranch yard, Bentley pulled up atop the hill directly above his ranch house. Bentley kept a close eye on Kittridge and his two ranch hands throughout the day. It was obvious to him that this was Kittridge's outfit. After learning all he needed to, he mounted up and headed back to the Maddox ranch. It was slow riding in the dark and he was a good eight hours out. He didn't want to take any unnecessary chances and have his horse break a leg. As a result, he didn't get back until almost four in the morning. Tired, he headed straight to the bunkhouse after putting his horse up. He needed sleep, and Vance could wait a few more hours before hearing what he has to report.

There was a knock on the door. Vance got up and opened it to find Bentley standing there.

"Mr. Vance,...".

"Stop. We can't talk here. I don't want anything we say or do to be overheard or seen by the ranch hands, or Maddox himself. Let's take a ride, we can talk out on the range."

"Alright boss."

When they reached the first stream, approximately a mile out from the ranch house, Vance stopped and dismounted. Bentley followed his lead.

"Alright Bentley, what did you learn?"

"He has his own ranch boss. He is trapping wild horses and breaking them. I think he is in love with that Strand woman. He spent Sunday night at her ranch. After returning to his own place, he packed for what looked to be an extended trip. I would have stayed and followed, but I returned as you instructed after finding where he was held up."

"You did right Bentley. During your surveillance did you happen to see any horses that looked like they didn't belong? You know, not Mustangs?"

"He has two large draft horses, which seemed a little out of place since he isn't doing any plowing. Also, he has two big blacks, I've never seen anything like them, but it's clear they aren't mustangs. They appear to be the same breed as the stallion he rode out on."

"Those are the one's I am talking about. Are you sure there were only two besides the stallion, and not three."

"If there is a third, it wasn't at his ranch."

"I want you to steal the two he's keeping in the barn. I have located a box canyon on the west section of the ranch. There are no other ranch activities taking place over there at this time. You can hold them in the back of the canyon, and no one will find you there."

"That's pretty risky boss, he has two Crow working for him, they seem to be at the ranch most all the time."

"Just sit and wait. Those ranch hands will have to tend to the mustangs and the cattle he keeps out in the pastures at sometime. When they do, slip down and grab the horses unseen. When I kill Kittridge, we'll take the stallion and the other two, and head west."

"Boss, why don't I just bushwhack him along the trail? There won't be any witnesses, so we can get away clean with no one the wiser."

"I don't just want him dead. If that was the case I would have had you kill him long before now. I want him starring up into my eyes when I fire the bullet into his head. I want him to know it's me, that it's personal for killing my brother."

"I don't know boss, any man that could best Tyrone, Robbie, and Pablo, all on the same night, that's not a man I would brace. Besides, his ranch is fledgling, he doesn't have any cash or gold per se. According to the hands here on the Maddox Ranch, those Crow only work for food and lodging only. So what can be gained by killing him?"

"I am not stupid Bentley, I'm not going to call him out to a gunfight. You just leave the details of killing him to me. In the meantime, without drawing to much attention to yourself, ask around and see if you can find out where Kittridge is headed. I need to know if he is going back to Eagle Creek."

They rode back to the ranch in silence. When they approached the main road, Vance headed back to the ranch, and Bentley rode to town.

Chapter 12

Corey rode all day non-stop, he wanted to reach the Powder River to camp for the night. Normally he wouldn't have traveled this direction, and especially would not have camped near the rivers edge. His friendship with Shadow Hawk has changed all that. He no longer fears an Indian attack while traveling through Sioux territory. Even so, he made camp inside the tree line. Farther south, when he reaches Cheyenne territory, it will be a whole different Story.

After making camp he poured a cup of coffee and let his thoughts drift back. He knows he should have stayed in Eagle Creek to clear his name instead of running. It was just that at the time, with Forest Vance having the Commanding Officer in his hip pocket, it seemed hopeless. Their allegiance was to strong for the sheriff and him to fight. Now his past has caught up with him and placed the one he loves in danger.

He had not told Alejandra of his plans to travel south. He believed his secret was safe with Jason. There was no reason for him to think Jason would tell Regina, and certainly, not that she would pass it on to Alejandra.

He drifted off somewhere in thought, sleeping through the night. The snap of the twig was loud, Corey was startled awake. It was a sound made by a heavy crushing weight. One only a human would make. He slowly circled his camp with his eyes as he laid perfectly still. He heard nothing more and no one was in sight. Careful not to make it noticeable, he rolled onto his side, giving him a direct line of sight to where he believed the sound had originated, it also gave him access to his pistol.

The sound of the intruder's voice was low as he spoke in a whisper.

"You are a careless man, this is the second time you have let me sneak up on you."

"This time is different, I can get to my pistol."

"That is why I stepped on the twig instead of just walking into your camp. I came to tell you your being watched."

"Please, come in and sit Shadow Hawk, I'll get the coffee started. Am I being watched now?"

"No. Returning from the hunt, I found where a man sat his horse and watched your place from the hill behind your house. It appears he spent the entire day watching, then left around sunset."

"How do you know he was there all day?"

"The number of smoke butts on the ground and the different stages of his horse's manure. A man that watches from hiding can only be up to no good."

Corey told Shadow Hawk his story about being arrested for killing the men that murdered his father. And how the towns people helped him escape. Then of his meeting Maddox. A man he had never met before, but who knew he was from Texas and on the run.

"Shadow Hawk, I think someone is hunting me. I need to return home and clear my name. If I don't, everyone I know and those around me will be in danger."

At that very instant, the log between Corey's feet exploded. Shattered by a .54 caliber bullet from a sharps buffalo gun. Shadow Hawk disappeared into the forest. Corey dove behind a large oak tree just as the second bullet streaked past his head.

Corey was at a disadvantage not having his rifle at hand. With the shooter using a Sharps, he could remain well out of pistol range. Just below his position was a thin trough that had been dug out by previous rains. It was just deep enough to cover Corey's movements.

Wanting to keep his attacker in place, Corey flashed a shoulder outside the oak tree, it worked, the shooter fired, but Corey had pulled back before the shooter could score a hit. The main thing was that the shooter believe he has Corey trapped with no escape.

Lying on his belly and keeping the oak between himself and the shooter, Corey slid down into the trough. lying flat on his belly he crawled for a good fifty yards. Then, very carefully, he removed his hat and raised his head, just high enough to get a look. Unable to locate his attacker, he slipped back down into the trough. He crawled another fifty yards before slipping out of the trough and up the hillside.

He still was unable to locate the bushwhacker. Judging from the crack of the first bullet, he estimated the shooter to be approximately 200 yards above his camp. He had now traveled approximately 250 yards up the hill, which should put him just about on line with his attacker, or slightly above him. Slowly he worked his way toward the shooter's position. Whispering to himself that he should be close.

It was then that he placed his hand down on a patch of wet leaves. Looking down to see why the leaves were wet, he picked his hand up to see it covered in blood. His thoughts raced through his head. *"Something isn't right. Why would this fresh blood be here? Unless maybe his attacker had taken the time to butcher some animal to eat while waiting. But it appeared to be to much blood to be a rabbit or other small animal."*

After wiping the blood on his trousers, Corey placed his hand on the butt of his pistol, expecting a shot from his attacker to pierce the air at anytime. Then the snapped twig, just as it had been earlier down below at camp. And just like earlier, Shadow Hawk spoke.

"It is okay my friend, he will track you no more."

"I owe you, Shadow Hawk."

"Forget it, I was just repaying the debt, for when you kept Panther from shooting me the first time we met."

"Can you tell me if this was the man spying on me back at the ranch?"

"This is not the same man. This man's horse is larger, and he also has a mule. Besides, why wait until you were in Sioux territory to shoot you. He could have done it so easily back at the ranch."

"You have a point. This means Maddox, or whoever told this man how to find me, is spreading the story of my being a wanted man. Others may be hunting me, also in hopes of collecting a bounty."

Shadow Hawk was concerned about Corey traveling such a far distance all alone through hostile territory.

"Your old home is two moons away, when do you plan on returning."

"I am hopeful I will be able to conduct my business at Fort Laramie, and not have to return all the way to Texas. Hopefully, I can turn myself in there and receive a fair hearing. One outside the influence of Forest Vance, the man behind all my troubles."

"Be careful my friend. The Cheyenne are very active. They are attacking the wagon trains along what the white man calls, the Oregon Trail. Just like the Sioux attack the wagon trains on the Bozeman Trail."

"I'll keep that in mind and travel more cautiously from here on. I'll return home if they don't hang me. Can't say for sure though how long I'll be gone. I would appreciate it if you could keep an eye on the ARMS Ranch and Alejandra for me. Make sure that whoever was watching me, does not turn his attention toward my friends."

"I will, it gives me a chance to see Skah."

They shook hands and parted ways. Corey picked up the dead man's guns and collected his horse and mule. The dead man appeared to be a buffalo hunter, and part time miner based on the way he was outfitted. He most likely heard the story of Corey be a fugitive while mining up around River Bend. Probably from someone working in the Maddox mine.

It was bad enough that Corey had a warrant out for his arrest. Now with Maddox spreading the word, bounty hunters were trying to kill him. It didn't matter that no one in the territory had any authority to arrest him, or that there wasn't even a wanted poster offering a reward.

Chapter 13

The owner of the trading post was telling a couple trappers about how his prostitute was taken from him by some woman. As he was recounting the story, another man was lingering around the firearms sipping whiskey. It wasn't until the post's owner said the woman was some blond bitch moving a herd of longhorns north that Trent showed an interest.

At the mention of a woman moving a herd north, the young man turned around and strolled over to the three men. Reaching out, he grabbed the owner by the arm and swung him around so he was facing him.

"Exactly where was this woman that stole your prostitute headed?"

Angry, Boone yelled at the young man to release his arm.

"Let go of me. Who do you think you are anyway?"

Pulling his pistol, Trent pressed it up under the man's chin.

"I am the man that is going to kill you if you don't answer my questions."

"Alright, don't get yourself all worked up. All she said, was that she was moving her herd up into the Montana Territory. That if I followed her, or tried to cause any trouble for the girl, she would kill me. I don't know anything else. Honestly. What is this woman to you anyway?"

"She is my future wife."

Holstering his gun, Trent released his hold on Boone.

"Did she ever tell you her name?"

"No, she never did."

"Describe her to me."

Boone still hadn't learned how to hold his tongue.

"If she's your future wife, why is it you don't you know what she looks like, or her name?"

Trent reached out, grabbing Boone by his throat and squeezed hard.

"If you value your ability to talk, you will tell me what she looked like. I want to make sure it's her. I don't want to go on a wild goose chase after the wrong woman."

To tell the truth, Trent already knew in his mind that it was Alejandra. No other woman would have the fortitude to take the prostitute from Boone.

Coughing while he spoke, as a result of Trent's grip around his throat, Boone described Alejandra.

"She was tall, maybe five foot eight inches tall, had long blond hair and green eyes. There were two other women with her, and an old Mexican."

Trent removed his hand from Boone's throat. Satisfied it was Alejandra, Trent saddled up and headed north. He knew about Regina, but he couldn't figure out who the other woman might be, unless it was the one from Big Springs that was raped by the buffalo hunters.

As Trent rode in solitude, he played back the events in his mind that led up to now, where he finds himself riding the outlaw trail.

Two years after shooting Alejandra's father, Trent assumed the responsibilities of managing the Oswald ranch. His father suffered a stroke. Incapacitating him for just over a year. However, unbeknownst to him, his father had kept certain papers, mostly personal items such as his will, marriage license, and birth certificates in a safe deposit box down at the bank. His father kept this box secret because it contained the deed to the Strand Ranch, which he never intended his son to see. The reason was that the deed included the actual purchase price.

It's been five years since Alejandra left Val Verde County, Texas, and Trent never got over the way she shunned him. He considered himself a man of wealth and influence, he couldn't understand how any woman, especially a dirt rancher like Alejandra could refuse him.

After selling a hundred head of cattle down at the stock yards Trent walked over to the bank to make a deposit. As he entered the bank, the Manager walked out of his office to greet him.

"Hello Trent, looks like the sale of beef to the army was profitable. By the way, considering your father's health, don't you think it would be wise to put your name on the safety deposit box?"

Trent was taken by surprise. His father had never mentioned ever having a safety deposit box. Being capable of not letting his emotions be known, Trent acted as if he knew about the box all along.

"You know Mr. Masters, I have been planning on doing that, I just haven't found the time to drop by and get it done. Why don't we take care of that now while I'm in town?"

"Great I'll get the signature card prepared. In the mean time, why don't you take a look inside the box. I'm familiar with all your fathers legal documents, so if you have any questions, feel free to ask. I should be able to clear up any questions you may have."

Trent shuffled through the papers, reading their titles, not bothering to read the specifics. He was finding nothing unusual, mostly standard family documents to include a will leaving him the ranch. Then he picked up the document at the bottom of the box. He couldn't believe what he was holding in his hand. It was the deed for the Strand Ranch.

Why had his father hid this document from him. He opened the document at the folds to read it in more depth. The first paragraph read.

"In consideration of Ten Thousand dollars, Alejandra Strand hereby sells the Strand Ranch to Lucas Oswald."

Trent was furious, he stormed out of the bank as he pushed Mr. Masters to the side as he inquired as to whether everything was alright.

Trent was dismounting as his horse was sliding on its haunches to a stop in the ranch yard. He hit the ground running and sprinted into the house, yelling for his father to come down. Fearful his son had been hurt, Lucas hurried down the stairs to see what all the commotion was about.

"Father, I've just returned from the bank. I found the deed of transfer for the Strand Ranch. You paid her ten thousand dollars, not five hundred like you told me. Why did you pay such an outrageous price for that worthless scrub land? More importantly, why did you lie to me?"

"Trent, I knew you would be upset about my paying Ms. Strand so much money, and I felt you would do something else you might regret."

"What do you mean something else?"

"I paid Alejandra that money as restitution for her fathers death. I found Eli's money pouch hidden away in your bedroom. I know it was you who murdered Eli Strand."

Trent snapped, without even thinking he drew his pistol and fired. His father laid dead on the floor of the parlor. The cook and house maid came running into the parlor from the kitchen to see what had happened. As they entered the room, Trent was standing over his father's body. His pistol still smoking from the shot that killed his father.

Trent turned and ran out of the house. Swinging into the saddle he spurred his horse and raced away. There was no escaping this killing. It wasn't some poor traveler, or squatter that could be wrote off as a rustler shot out on the plains. This time there were witnesses. No longer was Trent Oswald a man of means, he was a killer on the run.

He was determined to find Alejandra and force her to marry him. He wasn't quite sure how he would find her, and all he had to go on was that she moved the herd north when she left. So that's where he'd start, heading north to pick up her trail and talking with people that were around five years ago.

The story of the buffalo hunters at Big Springs was well known by everyone in the area. Even those who hadn't lived there five years ago knew the story. The Indians made sure they spread the word of how a woman bested the three buffalo hunters. How she staked them out naked and branded one across his chest.

As the story goes, the buffalo hunters pleaded with the Indians to spare their lives. In hopes that the Indians would show pity, they told them how six bandits had snuck up on their camp and forced them to strip out of their clothes or die. The problem was, the Indians had witnessed the whole episode from the rocks above, starting with the raping of the pioneer woman.

It didn't matter that there was no description of the woman. There was no question in Trent's mind that the woman who bested the hunters was Alejandra. From there he continued north into the Unorganized Territory. Not just because it was north, but because it was the most likely route for anyone to move a herd. She would want to travel someplace land was plentiful for the taking. Good land with access to water. Somewhere there would be little civilization, and little chance of there being overbearing cattle Barons like the Oswald's. Where else but the Indian territories to find such land and opportunity.

So it's not just by chance Trent found himself at the trading post in El Pueblo. Alejandra was always a striking, powerful woman. It isn't hard to follow a five year old trail such as hers. A woman of that caliber driving a herd of longhorns over 1,500 miles, and besting the men who wronged her, or her friends. That kind of woman and her deeds tend to last in the memories of those who have crossed her path, or were put in their place, for a long time. Without knowing it, Alejandra had become somewhat of a legend with the Rocky Mountain inhabitants.

Trent's horse stumbled, and he was quickly brought back to reality. Trent has never been mentally stable since killing his father. He has convinced himself that Alejandra is the blame for all his problems. If she had only agreed to marry him, none of this would ever have happened. Their fathers would still be alive, and they would be happily married, living as prominent citizens in Val Verde County.

Chapter 14

Corey crossed the Powder River and headed south for Fort Laramie. He wasn't all that happy about having to travel with the extra horse and mule he got from Spencer. Not only did they slow him down, the packs on the mule created more noise than he would have liked traveling through Cheyenne territory.

He stayed close to the base of the mountain to make travel faster and keep from silhouetting himself against the skyline. He knew if he cut east too soon and crossed the Belle Fourche River, it was far more likely that he would run into the Cheyenne or Arapaho near Devils Tower, (Bear Lodge, as it was known by the Cheyenne and Lakota Tribes).

With the sun starting to set, Corey rode up to the fork of the Powder River and Little Powder River. After watering the horses he moved well back into the forest. Before setting up camp, he searched for recent activity, such as cook fires and horse tracks, shod and unshod. Finding no evidence of recent activity, he dismounted and stripped the gear from the horses and mules. After giving Spirit a good rubdown, he quickly brushed the other horse and mules. Then walked all of them down to the Little Powder River to let them cool their legs and drink.

Corey contemplated the risk he was taking by going back and turning himself in to the Army. While it's true Forest Vance most likely wielded no influence in Fort Laramie. There was also no one there to provide evidence that the killings were justified, or that Tyrone Vance drew first. Still, Corey felt his chances were much better in Fort Laramie than returning to Eagle Creek and mounting a defense against Forest Vance with all his wealth and influence. Not to mention having the Colonel commanding Fort Arbuckle in his hip pocket.

If Corey had only knew what transpired after his escape, he would be lying in bed wrapped in Alejandra's arms back at the ranch. Instead, he was squatting in the forest without a fire to keep warm or heat a pot of coffee. Pulling a piece of jerky from his pack, he decided to go through the buffalo hunters pack as he chewed on the dry salted meat, and see what might be useful.

Although there were newer models, the Sharps Cory took off Spencer was relatively new itself, made in 1853. There were cartridges and extra pellets primers. The pellet primers replaced the tape primers which were susceptible to moisture and caused misfires. The pack included many of the staples any traveler would have, coffee, flour, beans, and fatback. On one side of the pack saddle was mining equipment. It was at the bottom of this pack that he found a small pouch with a waded piece of paper stuck in the bottom.

Corey removed the paper and pressed it out with his hands. It was dark now and to difficult to read the writing. Having been distracted by the paper, he took a few minutes to listen for any hostiles that might be sneaking up on his camp. Aside from the normal night sounds of the forest, there didn't seem to be any other movements. Taking a chance, he lit a match so he could read the paper.

"Spencer, his name is Kittridge, he stands six foot four, has black hair and rides a big grey stallion. He is wanted for murder in Texas. Remember we split the reward 50/50.

Bentley."

Not paying attention, the match burned down and burnt Corey's finger. He threw the match to the ground and sucked on his finger to cool the burn and ease the pain.

Corey was thinking to himself, *"Bentley, who is Bentley? He obviously isn't working for Maddox."* Unable to place the name, he checked the rest of Spencer's mining supplies and pack. He couldn't find anything to give him a clue as to Bentley's identity.

Wanting to get an early start, Corey rolled out his bed roll. It wasn't long before he was fast asleep. Waking up, he could feel he was being watched. And whoever it was seemed to be inside the camp. Slowly, not to alert his visitor to his motions, he slipped his hand down to his pistol, which was lying on the ground under the blanket.

He sat up quickly, simultaneously throwing his blanket off and cocking the hammer of his pistol. Corey pointed the gun at a man standing over a fire and warming his hands with a hot cup of coffee.

"Mister, if I was you, I'd move almighty careful. Turn around, slowly, and just keep your hands wrapped around that cup."

"Man you are one sound sleeper. Put that gun away, I could have killed you five times over already."

"Jason, what are you doing here?"

"Good morning to you too. Alejandra and Regina sent me. They didn't much like the idea of you traveling all alone through hostile Indian territory. They also thought you should have a friend in Fort Laramie when you turned yourself in to the law. If something goes wrong and you are placed in jail to hang. Someone needs to be there to send for help."

"How..."

"Sky spoke with Shadow Hawk, who told her of the ambush. Then she told Alejandra. Turns out she already knew you were wanted for killing Tyrone Vance, who murdered your father. She had no idea, however, you had rode off to turn yourself in, like an idiot. That's her word not mine."

"I know it doesn't make sense Jason, but I have to clear my name if anyone around me is to remain safe. As you Know, there has already been an attempt on my life. By the way, do you know a man named Bentley?"

"Never heard of him. Is he the one who tried to bushwhack you back on the Bighorn River?"

"No, turns out his name was Spencer, just an old buffalo hunter and miner. He was acting on instructions from this Bentley character."

"I rode hard for a day and a half without stopping for sleep, and used up my horse getting here. Mind if I get some shut eye before we ride on."

"Go ahead. I'm going to bury this mining gear, it will lighten the load and we will make a whole lot less noise. I'll take the horses down to the river and give yours a good brushing."

Corey turned to thank Jason for making the coffee, but Jason was already asleep. As he attended to the horses, he let his thoughts drift back to Alejandra. He was relieved that she knew about his killing Tyrone Vance and his two gunmen.

Corey was thankful their romance has blossomed, even with her having known about his past this whole time. Therefore, she must believe him innocent of murder and that the killings were justified. Getting to know Alejandra over the past year has taught him that she would never condone the killing of anyone in cold blood.

When the horses had filled their bellies, Corey returned to camp buried the mining supplies and loaded up the pack animals. He had just finished saddling the horses when Jason woke up. It has been six hours since Jason had fell asleep.

"There are some biscuits and fatback in the frying pan."

"Thanks, any of that coffee left?"

"Enough for one cup."

Corey cleaned and packed the frying pan and coffee pot as Jason ate.

"Corey, are you sure you wouldn't rather turn back and give up this notion of clearing your name. You know you can't be arrested in the territory for any crimes you might have committed in Texas."

"I need to do this, not just for myself, but for Alejandra, and all the rest of you too. Ready to ride?"

"You bet. You know your going to make some woman a good wife."

They both chuckled.

"Go rinse that tin plate off and stuff it in your saddle bags. You can ride the horse I got off Spencer. We'll let yours rest today from the hard ride you put him through yesterday."

They broke camp and headed out just after noon. They rode in silence for most of the day, keeping a sharp eye out for Indians. By the time they reached the end of the Little Powder River, it was time to make camp for the night. The terrain was rocky, and had far less forest to provide cover.

"Jason, ride up into that stand of boulders off to your right and see if there is an opening large enough to make camp and hide the horses."

Jason wheeled his horse and pushed him up the side of the hill. When he reached the boulders he was shocked to find a huge flat open area. It was large enough to accommodate them and the livestock, with plenty of room to move about under cover. He waived for Corey to come up.

Corey picketed the mules and Jason's horse on the rivers edge so they could drink and wade in the river. Catching up the reins to Spirit he swung into the saddle without ever touching the stirrups. Once up the hill, he dismounted and led Spirit in behind the boulders. Looking back down to the river he was pleased with their campsite. It was well hidden and provided excellent protection.

"You choose, do you want to cook, or take care of the stock?"

"Your the horse whisperer, I'll cook."

Once again the two laughed. Grabbing the reins to his stallion and Spencer's horse, Corey went back down to the river. As he was unsaddling the horses, three Cheyenne Dog Soldiers rode up behind him. They had walked their horses up in the soft sand, allowing them to close within thirty yards of Corey before he knew they were there. They were now well within range of their bows, and nobody had to tell Corey they wouldn't miss at this range. He was hopeful Jason had noticed them and was covering him with his rifle.

Corey slid the saddle off his horse and laid it down on the bank. Then he started to rub down the horse like nothing was wrong. As if they were friends, Corey looked up at the Cheyenne braves and raised his free hand, palm out. The universal sign to signify he was a friend.

Jason had not noticed the Cheyenne warriors until after they had stopped in front of Corey. He was just starting to light the camp fire when he glimpsed them out of the corner of his eye. He was now crouched behind the boulders, watching what was happening down at the river.

Corey was in his line of fire, and Jason didn't have a clear shot. At best, he might be able to pick off the one on his far right. All he could do at this point was watch, and hope Corey could talk his way out. He did notice that sometime since the Indians had arrived, Corey managed to slip the leather thong off the hammer of his pistol. It had been so subtle, no one, including Jason, had noticed. Jason wondered how he'd missed the move.

The conversation was starting to get loud, a bad sign when Indians are involved. Two of the Braves had notched their arrows. Any wrong move now and Corey would be a dead man.

With his focus on Corey, Jason was unaware the Indians had raised their bows, and were prepared to shoot. In response he started to raise his rifle. But before he could bring the rifle up to his shoulder, all three Indians had been shot off their horses and were lying in the dirt. Two were dead, the third was gasping for breath with a bullet in his lungs. It happened so fast, Jason never even saw Corey go for his pistol. Yet, he had drawn and shot all three before Jason could even take aim with his rifle. Jason sprinted down from the boulders.

"Corey, are you alright?"

"I'm fine. Mount up and grab those ponies. We can't let them return to the main war party."

"How do you know there are more."

"These are Cheyenne Dog Soldiers. They never travel in small numbers, except for their scouts. Now round up those ponies and get them up behind the boulders."

As Jason rounded up the Indian ponies, Corey got their own horses and mules back up behind the boulders. The campsite was perfect. It provided plenty of cover, with space for Corey and Jason to move around unseen. In addition, there was a huge canopy carved out under the cliff to protect the horses.

After Jason retuned with the ponies, Corey gathered all the canteens, including the one off Spencer's horse and the leather water pouches off the ponies. He slipped down to the river, and filled the water pouches and canteens, then wiped out their tracks to and from the river, along with those leading up to the boulders. The extra water would be needed if they came under attack by the main war party.

Before the sun set, they finished eating a couple rabbits they shot earlier. Extinguishing the camp fire they sat in silence as night fell.

"Jason, you take the first four hours. I'll take the watch the last four."

Jason was pleased to take the first watch. The second was always the worst for trying to stay alert and remain awake. Around the third hour into his watch

Jason began to replay the events of the day in his mind. *"I cannot remember seeing Corey draw or shoot. By the time I raised my rifle, the shooting was over, and the Indians laid dead in the dirt. It appeared as if Corey was never concerned about the danger he faced. I was of no help, yet he hasn't once questioned what I had been doing, or why I didn't fire a single shot. He merely went about the business of cleaning up the scene and getting ready for another attack. Could it be that he really is a cold blooded killer."*

Corey walked up behind Jason while he was still in deep thought. Startled, Jason jumped to his feet.

"You alright Jason?"

"Yeah, I'm fine. It's all quiet, you startled me is all."

"Good, let's hope it stays quiet."

Corey could tell something was bothering Jason, and most likely it was the speed and skill in which he dispatched of the dog soldiers.

Early the next morning while the sky was still grey, Corey cared for the horses, and packed the mules before waking Jason. The sun was creeping over the horizon when Corey walked over to Jason's bed roll and nudged him with his boot toe.

"Jason, how about a cup of coffee and some jerky? I had to keep the fire small enough just to heat coffee. I couldn't risk frying up bacon for fear of sending up a smoke trail and attracting unwanted guests."

"I understand, thanks."

Corey didn't want yesterday's events to come between him and Jason. He considered Jason his friend, and he could tell Jason was uncomfortable with him after yesterday's encounter with the Cheyenne.

"Jason, I would like to talk to you about what happened yesterday and back in Texas. Would that be alright?"

"I am not sure I want to know Mr. Kittridge."

"Mr. Kittridge is it? Jason, I grew up in Northern Mexico, now known as the Republic of Texas. We had to deal with Mexican bandits, Comanche, Cheyenne, and Comancheros. Not to mention rustlers and the like. I practiced religiously every day perfecting my quick draw. Not to become a bully and run rough shod over others, but to protect my family and friends. I'm sorry if my actions yesterday scared you. I had no choice but to kill those Cheyenne. It was either them or us. I realize I didn't allow any time for mourning, but we had to reset quickly and prepare for another attack. There was no time to feel sorrow for those who died. What have you heard about what I did back in Texas?"

"Aside from you outdrawing three men, one of which murdered your father, it is being said by some that you didn't give Tyrone Vance or his men a chance to defend themselves. I hadn't ever thought you capable of killing someone in cold blood. But after yesterday, it makes me question what really did happen back in Texas."

"I can understand you having doubts. You really don't know much about me, other than what I've told you during the limited time we rode together on the ARMS Ranch. I can tell you those men killed my father, and five of our Vaqueros, while rustling our herd. Don't let anyone convince you otherwise. I let each one of those men I killed draw first. In fact, I faced Vance's two gun hands, Robbie and Pablo, at the same time. Even then, at a disadvantage facing two men at once, I allowed them to draw first. Why would I risk hanging if I didn't feel my actions were justified. Regardless of whether you believe me or not, I promise, you have nothing to fear from me. If you prefer, you can turn back and head home. I wouldn't blame you in the least, and I won't hold it against you if you do return."

"Corey, I apologize for doubting you. Truth is, I feel safer with you, and don't wish to be out there alone. Now that you have explained what happened in Texas, I believe you acted honorably in seeking retribution against those who murdered your father. It's just, well, I never saw anyone with such speed and accuracy with a pistol. To be honest, it scared me. Those I've seen that have even come close to drawing as quick as you, have all been outlaws."

"I'm glad to have your trust in me back. More importantly, to have you calling me Corey again, instead of Mr. Kittridge. Believe me Jason, I didn't want to kill those Cheyenne. I had no other choice, it was either them or us."

Riding side by side, Corey told Jason the rest of his story, how Forest Vance used his influence with the Commanding Officer of Fort Arbuckle to have the sheriff's ruling of self defense overturned.

Around noon, Corey used the Sharps he acquired from Spencer to shoot a deer. The shot measured close to three hundred yards. It gave him a good chance to familiarize himself with the weapon. He might be in need of it in the future. After having a couple large steaks and biscuits, they smoked and jerked the remaining meat, then rode on.

Hearing the full story, Jason was confident Corey was innocent of murder. Once again he considered him a close friend. Thankful Corey was on his side after seeing him in action. Three weeks later they rode into Fort Laramie.

"Jason, what say we stop off at the saloon for a cold beer first. I'm buying, it may be a long time before I get the chance to enjoy your company or a cold beer again."

They were chuckling as they walked through the bat wing doors of the saloon.

"Bartender, two cold beers and whiskey."

"You want a beef steak and some potatoes to go along with that?"

"You bet we would, we've been riding close to a month, and eating mighty little as a result of little or no camp fires."

The bartender looked at them in amazement.

"Four weeks and your still alive? Don't you two know the Cheyenne are on the warpath."

"We know now, we ran into a few of them along the way."

"Major Wainwright is going to want to speak with you two boys. He's out on patrol right now, but he'll be back in a couple hours."

Corey's heart sank. Major Wainwright was second in command at Fort Arbuckle when he killed Tyrone.

The bartender brought the bottle over to the table.

"Son, are you sure you can handle this who shot John?"

Corey yanked the bottle and glasses out of the bartender's hands.

"Don't worry about me old timer, just bring those cold beers and the chow."

"I didn't mean to offend you son."

"I'm sorry, I just got some bad news, and unfairly took it out on you."

He gave the bartender a dollar tip for his service.

Corey poured Jason a drink and told him about Major Wainwright being at Fort Arbuckle. Along with his reservations now about receiving a fair hearing in Fort Laramie. The frown on his face and anger he showed toward the bartender, made it difficult for Corey to tell whether Corey wanted to stay at the Fort, or continue on to Eagle Creek.

"What do you want to do Corey, ride out or stay and fight? You don't strike me as being the type of man to cut and run when the going get's tough. If you are truly innocent, stand up and fight for yourself. You don't have to face this all by yourself. You have friends now, including me. I'll do whatever you ask. If you need me to ride to Eagle Creek and bring back witnesses, I'll do it."

"Thanks Jason, lets see what Major Wainwright has to say first. If he doesn't believe me maybe you'll have to ride to Eagle Creek, but I don't want you riding this territory alone. You would be in danger from both the Indians and Forest Vance."

They sat in silence while eating their steak and potatoes and downing their second cold beer. Strangers came and went, all of them sizing up the two men sitting at the corner table. The story of them surviving a trip through Cheyenne territory drew the interest of everyone in the fort. It was another thirty minutes before the Sargent entered the saloon.

"Is there a Mr. Kittridge in here?"

Corey pushed his chair back and stood up to face the Sargent.

"I'm Kittridge."

"Sir, please come with me. Major Wainwright would like to have a word with you regarding your travels through Cheyenne territory."

"Is it alright if my partner tags along?"

Jason snapped his head up, proud of the fact Corey called him his partner.

"Sure, lets go."

Corey and Jason followed the Sargent over to the headquarters building.

"Wait here."

The Sargent disappeared into an office shutting the door behind him. Minutes later the door opened and the Sargent reappeared.

"The Major will see you now."

The Major's congenial demeanor surprised Corey.

"Mr. Kittridge, I'm glad to see you. There aren't many men who travel through Cheyenne territory and live to talk about the experience. I am hoping you will be of some assistance in helping me understand their movements. I would also like to hear about any encounters you had with them directly."

Corey was totally caught off guard, he had prepared himself to be arrested the moment in stepped into the Major's office.

"Yes sir, I would be pleased to help you in any way I can. First, I would like to discuss a personal matter. One I know you'll be familiar with from your station at Fort Arbuckle. I have traveled here to turn myself in for the killing of Tyrone Vance and his two gun hands, Robbie and Pablo. It is important to me that I clear my name, and put the matter behind me."

"Mr. Kittridge, I thought you knew. You were exonerated of all charges levied against you. Shortly after your escape, the killing was reinvestigated and it was determined you acted in self defense. Your actions were deemed justifiable in the apprehension of a known criminal. The investigation was conducted by the regional magistrate at the behest of the citizens of Eagle Creek and the Cattleman's Association. The investigation found the Vance brothers guilty of rustling, and a warrant has been issued for the arrest of Forest Vance. The Commanding Officer of Fort Arbuckle was found guilty of collusion and taking bribes. He was then court martialed and given a dishonorable discharge."

"Major, I have been living in the Montana Territory since my escape. I had no way of knowing."

"I am truly sorry for the loss of your father, and any inconvenience the Army caused you. Your father was a good friend of mine. I wish I could have done more for you at the time. Most of the officers at the fort never believed you committed those killings in cold blood. Never the less, I am sure you can sympathize with my position. As an officer in the U. S. Army, I am bound to follow the orders of my Commanding Officer, regardless of my personal feelings as to their appropriateness."

"Thank you Major. I don't mind telling you, I was more than a little a bit concerned when I learned you were the Fort's Commanding Officer. I wasn't sure if I could receive a fair hearing or not. It's comforting to know we have honorable men, such as yourself, serving in the Army. Now, let's discuss the Cheyenne."

After Corey finished recounting the run in he and Jason had with the Cheyenne Dog Soldiers. They spent several hours discussing strategies on how to fight the Cheyenne. Most of them based on his experience fighting the Cheyenne and Comanche in Texas. At the conclusion of their talks, the Major offered Corey one last piece of advice.

"Mr. Kittridge, Forest Vance was never arrested. It's widely believed, that he fled to Sante Fe. Regardless of where he fled to, I would keep an eye on my back trail if I was you. He carries a lot of hate for you killing his brother. It wouldn't surprise me if he wanted to get revenge for his brothers death."

"I'll keep that in mind Major. Can you recommend a good place we can spend the night?"

The Major instructed a couple of men to take care of their belongings and tend to their horses, then he asked the Sargent to put them up in the empty officer's quarters. They accepted the Major's hospitality and were escorted to an empty cabin.

The Major made a point of wanting Corey to stop by and speak with him before heading home. Corey assured him they would stop by his office before leaving the Fort. After a couple weeks of dodging Indians, and going with little sleep as a result of standing guard all night, they both slept well past eight o'clock. The sun had been up for two hours by the time they opened their eyes.

Chapter 15

Corey and Jason went to the saloon and ordered a healthy breakfast, 4 eggs, biscuits with jam, and a thick slice of ham each, along with a hot pot of coffee. During breakfast, a short man entered the saloon and crossed over to their table.

"Mr. Kittridge this message just came across the wire for you. At least I think it's for you, it actually has your fathers first name instead of yours."

"I'll take it, thank you."

Corey handed the man a half dollar and opened the envelope encasing the message. He read the message as the telegraph operator walked away.

"Matthew- Stop. Mares stolen, Panther and Bear okay- Stop. Signed - Rusty- End."

"Jason, let's go see the Major. We need to ride, there's trouble back at the ranch."

After leaving the Major's office, Corey walked over to the telegraph office. He sent a message to Alejandra through Rusty. The message let her know he had been cleared of all charges, and both he and Jason are fine and headed home.

Corey led the way with each of them leading a mule packed with supplies. Corey sold Spencer's horse, as they had no need for it, and it helped purchase supplies for the trip home. Including an additional five boxes of ammunition.

As they passed through the gate, Corey dropped back to speak with Jason.

"What do you think Jason, should we follow the Oregon and Bozeman Trails all the way home, or return the way we came?"

"Well, we know for certain the Cheyenne are raiding the wagon trains along both Trails. We only ran into those three scouts the way we came. I vote for retracing the path we came."

"I agree. I believe the Cheyenne will be raiding farther west along the southern portion of the Bozeman Trail, where it crosses the Powder River. With any luck, we can make it through without crossing their path."

The first day was uneventful, as would be expected being sot close to the fort, even on the Oregon Trail. Other than themselves, there wasn't a single person or wagon traveling the Oregon Trail. Close to sundown they left the trail for good. They continued on for about a mile to the east before making camp.

The next few days travel was quiet. They now rode approximately fifty yards apart, keeping a close watch out for any sign of hostile Indians.

They had been on the trail close to two weeks now and hadn't encountered a single soul. It was late afternoon when they turned due north and headed for the Belle Fource River. The place Corey feared the most of running into the Cheyenne. They were about two miles out from the River and stopping for the night when eight Cheyenne Dog Soldiers rode out of a draw and charged them, screaming like banshees.

"Jason, ride for the river and find us a place we can defend, make sure the river is at our backs."

Jason spurred his horse into a dead run. Dropping the lead rope to his mule. The mule would follow, it was to slow to keep the fast pace loaded down with its heavy pack. Jason turned his head to see if Corey was following, he couldn't believe what he was seeing.

Corey reined up and dismounted. He quickly pulled the Sharps off his pack mule. Then he slapped the mule on the ass with the rifle, sending him after Jason's mule. Placing his foot on Spirit's reins, Corey knelt down, and placed a round in the breech of the sharps as he did so. Taking little time to aim, he fired. The lead rider fell from the saddle some 300 yards out. Calmly, Corey loaded another round in the breech. After squeezing the trigger, he quickly reloaded without looking to see if his second shot had found it's mark, he knew it had. They were closing the distance fast, Corey squeezed off another shot, dropping a third Indian.

Grasping the saddle horn with his free hand, Corey swung into the saddle as Spirit was already reaching speed. Jason was waving frantically to alert him to his position. From the looks of it, Jason had selected an excellent spot to stand and fight. As Corey dropped from his saddle, Spirit ran into the trees to join the other horse and mules. The remaining Dog Soldiers were unable to close the distance on Corey, Spirit was too fast. Still a 100 yards out, Corey took aim once again with the sharps. The result was the same as before, another Cheyenne lie dead in the dust.

Quickly Corey sprinted for the trees while Jason laid down cover fire. The Cheyenne broke off the charge and disappeared into the landscape. Jason ceased firing after Corey reached their stronghold.

"Man that was some shooting. I thought you were only good with a pistol."

"Actually my father taught me how to shoot with a rifle first. He wanted to make sure I could hunt, and keep the advantage against my attackers by keeping them pinned down from a distance. The Indians always outnumbered us, so it was important they not get close enough to overpower us with their superior numbers. I took the pistol up on my own."

"Well, you certainly evened up the odds. By my count you killed four. Leaving four more out there in the woods. You have any ideas of how we're going to take care of them?"

"Right now we are in a pretty good position. We have the water to our backs for protection and drinking, and it should be dark soon."

"So is that true what they say about Indians not attacking at night?"

"No, those who let their guard down believing that, are dead. Let's be quiet now. They are excellent in the woods, and unless they make a mistake, we won't hear them coming. Odds are we will be fighting hand to hand before the night's over."

They remained quiet, straining to pick up any sound out of the ordinary, like a snapped twig or brush of leather against a limb. Jason gave out a low gasp as the stone Corey threw hit his shoulder. Corey held up his knife, indicating Jason should pull his and be prepared to fight in close.

Just as Jason rolled over onto his side to draw his knife, a brave jumped through the bush pinning him to the ground. As the Indian readied to slash Jason's throat, Corey blew a hole in the Indian's head. Then as a second Indian jumped on top of Jason, Corey was tangling with the other two. They had jumped him right after he shot the first one off Jason.

It was mere luck, that the first Indian who jumped Corey didn't kill him. With his pistol knocked from his hand, Corey moved his hands in between his body and the Indian's by instinct, to keep the Indian's weight from knocking the air from his lungs. The Indian landed right on top the 12 inch blade of Corey's knife, cutting clear through his heart. The body laid limp on top of Corey, preventing the second Indian from being able to stab Corey. Reaching out to his left, Corey grabbed his pistol and fired point blank into the Indian's face.

Jason was wounded, but he was able to fight off his second attacker and kill him.

"Are you alright Jason?"

"I have a couple bad cuts, but I should live thanks to you. By my count you killed seven, and I only killed one. If it hadn't been for you shooting this one in the head, my throat would be cut and I'd be lying here dead."

"Remember, if it wasn't for my problems to begin with, you wouldn't have even been in this situation. So no thanks are necessary."

"All the same, I'm grateful."

"Let me have a look at those wounds. This one in your lower back is pretty nasty. You were lucky he missed your kidney. I'll have to sew it up. You think you can get some water boiling while I dig out some bandages and sewing thread."

"Sure, you will be gentle with me, won't you?"

Jason has a way of always making Corey laugh, even in a difficult situation as this.

The cut to Jason's lower back took fourteen stitches. He had a couple others that required two and four stitches. Aside from that he was only badly bruised.

Jason laid back on his bed roll to rest while Corey got some salt pork out of the packs to cook for dinner. Corey had to wake Jason up to eat, it was important Jason ate to keep up his strength.

"Jason, I'll keep watch all night."

"I can hold up my end. Just wake me when it's my turn."

"I know you can, but it is more important that you rest. It's going to be a long day tomorrow and your going to need all the strength you can muster."

Jason was fast asleep before Corey had even cleaned their plates. Corey packed everything up in case they had to move quick. Using the mules, Corey dragged the dead bodies far away from the camp and covered then with branches and leaves. He hoped it would be some time before the buzzards started to swarm and attract more Indians.

Jason's cut was worse off than Corey had led Jason to believe. It was going to be slow traveling from here on, and if they got into another fight with the Cheyenne, Jason was going to be of no help. Corey was hopeful of making it to the Little Powder today. Had it not been for Jason's injuries it wouldn't have been a problem.

Tired from no sleep, Corey set about his business with the sun rising. He put some water on to boil for cleaning Jason's wounds. Then he sliced some fat back for frying and rolled some biscuits. The smell and sizzling of the bacon frying woke Jason. As he tried to sit up, he wrenched in pain. Quickly getting Corey's attention.

"Lie back down Jason, I'll bring you a plate."

"You should just leave me Corey, you can make it out alive without having to worry about me."

"That's enough of that kind of talk, and I don't want to hear anymore. We'll make it out together, or not at all. Now eat up, you need the nourishment to keep up your strength. We have a long hard day's ride ahead of us."

Jason was feeling ashamed for having thought the worst of Corey after that first encounter with the Dog Soldiers. Now here they were with him in serious trouble, and Corey was fussing all over him. Putting his own life at risk when he could very easily ride off and save himself, and no one would have been the wiser.

Corey rigged up a back rest and attached it to Jason's saddle. After packing the mules, he carried Jason over to his horse and lifted him onto the saddle. Then strapped him to the backrest with his rope, leaving Jason's arms free to handle the reins, and a gun if necessary.

Corey kept them inside the tree line, maintaining a slow pace so Jason's wounds wouldn't rip open. They made it to the mouth of the Little Powder about two hours after sundown. Corey left Jason sitting his horse inside a stand of oak trees, while he rode forward to make sure the river was clear of any hostiles.

They had been there, but because of the slow pace set by Corey, they missed them by about three hours. Most likely they were now camped on the banks of the Powder River to the west. Even so, Corey went back to pick up Jason, then they traveled another hour north upriver before stopping. There was no need to tempt fate and camp in the same place Indians were using.

It took two more days just to get to the fork where the Little Powder and Powder Rivers met. It was of some relief though, because they were now in Sioux territory, with little chance of encountering anymore Cheyenne.

Jason was very weak from the infection that had set in and a loss of blood. He needed more medical attention than Corey could give him. As he was boiling water to change Jason's bandages, he heard that familiar snapped twig.

"Come on in Shadow Hawk."

"You remembered."

"Yes, and I couldn't be happier to see you. Jason is in a bad way. He needs medical attention if he is going to live. I did the best I could, but I'm afraid it isn't enough."

"You camp here, I will go for our Medicine Man. These two braves will remain here for your protection."

Shadow Hawk disappeared into the forest.

Corey wasn't really sure of where the Sioux's main camp was located, or how long it would take Shadow Hawk to return with help. It was two and half days before Shadow Hawk returned with the Medicine Man. It helped that Shadow Hawk had looked at Jason's wounds before he left, so the Medicine Man brought the proper herbs, salves, and potions he needed to treat the wound.

There was no more moving Jason until his wounds were better. his worst wound had turned septic and he was in danger of dying from blood poisoning. Shadow Hawk had sent word to the ARMS Ranch to let them know Corey and Jason have been delayed and would be arriving later than expected.

Although no particulars were provided to the warrior carrying the message. Regina and Alejandra both feared their man was injured, possibly dying. What else could keep them from returning home.

Both women raced into the house after receiving the message. Acting independently, and not knowing what the other was thinking, they prepared to ride hard and fast. They each strapped on their gun belt, filled the empty loops in their holster with bullets, and checked the loads in their guns. Grabbing their rifles, they ran into each other in the hallway. Quickly they scanned each other and smiled as they turned and hurried to the barn. Rusty didn't have to be told, he saddled their horses and had them tied to the rail well before the women came out of the house. He also prepared a pack horse with provisions to last five days.

Chapter 16

It was a two day ride to the Powder River where Shadow Hawk's messenger had said Corey and Jason were camped. The way the two women were riding, you would have thought they were trying to make it in one day. Upon reaching the Tongue River, they stopped to water the horses.

It was Alejandra that spoke up.

"Regina, it won't do us any good to continue on at this pace. All we'll do is kill our horses. Then we'll be no good to anyone."

"You're right. Besides, there could be any number of reasons other than being injured, that could be keeping them from returning to the ranch."

"Exactly, we are probably over reacting because we haven't seen them for so long. Let's camp here next to the river tonight."

Alejandra stripped the horses and walked them in the river to cool down. Regina started the coffee and put on a pot of beans, to which she added some salt pork.

After dinner, Regina turned in while Alejandra stood watch. The best she could tell, it was around two in the morning, so Alejandra woke Regina up to stand watch. The evening pasted without incident. The women were more concerned about unscrupulous white men trying to molest them, than an Indian attack.

They didn't bother with breakfast. As soon as it was light, they were in the saddle, and headed for the Powder River. It was mid afternoon when they found the camp. Regina saw Jason lying on his bed roll that was covered in blood. Jumping down from her horse, she ran over to his side. She knelt down and kissed his forehead. Crying as she looked up at Corey.

"What happened? The last we heard you were both fine when you left Fort Laramie."

"The Cheyenne are raiding up and down the Oregon and Bozeman Trails. We ran into eight Dog Soldiers at the Belle Fource River. The last four we fought hand to hand. Jason was very brave and fought well. I am sorry he had to place himself in danger on my account."

Alejandra was holding onto Corey's arm, squeezing it tight, as to never let him go. After Regina returned her focus to Jason, she whispered in Corey's ear.

"That was very nice of you. Shadow Hawk told me the whole story."

Jason has been unconscious for most of the last five days. Only when the Medicine Doctor forced him awake to drink his medicine, was he aware of his surroundings. The day after the women arrived, Jason woke early and seemed to be alert and aware of his surroundings.

Shadow Hawk approached Corey.

"The medicine made from cactus juice and other herbs have worked. The poison has left his body, and he should be okay to travel. As long as you take it easy. Make sure he doesn't open his wounds."

The Medicine Man changed the poultice covering the wounds to fight infection. Then he handed Corey a pouch full of extra poultice and gave him instructions.

"Make sure you keep it wet and change it every night."

"I can't thank you enough Shadow Hawk. Jason would have died had it not been for you and your

Medicine Man. If ever I can be of help to you, please send for me."

After the Sioux left, Corey and Alejandra began packing and saddling the horses. Since they now had three mules and the supplies had dwindled from use, Corey packed all the supplies and split the load between one mule and Jason's horse.

"Why are you putting a pack on Jason's horse? Surely you don't expect him to sit atop a mule."

"I'm making a travois to hang between the two remaining mules like a hammock. Jason will be able to lie down in the hammock, making the ride more comfortable than being dragged along the rough ground, or sitting in the saddle."

Alejandra stood on her tip toes and kissed Corey on the cheek.

"Is there nothing you can't do? You continue to amaze me, you're always thinking of others first, putting your own desires and needs last."

Blushing, Corey turned away and got back to making the travois. By the time he finished mounting it to the two sawbuck pack saddles, the women had the horses staged and ready.

Corey was standing over Jason, and the girls moved to help him get Jason Loaded. But before they could get there, Corey had Jason cradled in his arms.

"Regina, move to the front of the mules. As I place Jason on the travois, you place your arms under his shoulders and pull him forward, making sure you keep his head up."

Alejandra tried to hand Corey the reins to Spirit. He refused to take the reins and continued to maintain his hold on the lead ropes to the mules. With Jason resting easy in the hammock, Corey led them out, walking the mules. He wanted to control the pace and the spacing between the mules to reduce the stress placed on the hammock.

As they were leaving, Corey instructed Alejandra to mount up on Spirit, to use him and Midnight, and ride non-stop back to the ranch. Then bring back a wagon. Switching between her mare and Spirit, to keep them fresh, she traveled twice as fast.

Midmorning of the second day, Alejandra met them on the trail with the wagon. She had traveled with an extra team, switching them as she had her horses. She also brought three ranch hands with her to help.

While the men got Jason transferred into the wagon, Regina spoke with Alejandra.

"I offered to walk the mules on a couple of occasions to let Corey ride and rest his legs. He wouldn't have it, he feels responsible for Jason almost dying. And to think, you almost let him get away."

"Don't remind me. My first impressions of him couldn't have been more wrong."

With Jason loaded, Corey hopped into the back of the wagon to help keep him comfortable. Switching back and forth between the two teams, they made good time and arrived back at the ranch shortly after dark.

Corey carried Jason up to the main house and took him straight to the guest bedroom. After they had him resting comfortable, Corey headed out to the bunkhouse.

Alejandra followed him out of the room to the front door.

"Where do you think you're going mister?"

"Well, with Jason in the guest room, there isn't room for me in the main house. I'll sleep in the bunkhouse."

"The hell you will. Sunday is only two days away and we are going to church. I refuse to accept any more excuses for not getting married. You will sleep in my bedroom with me. I know you are tired from your hard trip. So go upstairs, get in bed, and get some sleep. I will be up later to check on you."

"Fine, but don't think just because we are getting married, that you can order me around all the time."

Alejandra smiled, and pushed him forward.

"Good, now get upstairs and get some sleep."

Chapter 17

Sunday arrived and Jason was back on his feet. He was walking slow, but he was walking. He stood in as Corey's best man, and Regina was Alejandra's maid of honor. Octavio gave the bride away.

The whole town and all the other ranchers turned out for the wedding. The only ones who didn't come were Forest Vance and Bentley. Corey still had no idea Vance was in River Bend. Vance wanted to keep it that way. It was now widely known that Corey had been cleared of murder, so Vance was forced to change his plans. Corey was being hailed a hero for his actions against the Cheyenne and for saving Jason's life.

Alejandra couldn't have been happier. Over the last five years she had all but given up on finding a man that could live up to her father. Now she had a loving husband who had the same morals and values as Eli Strand. She considered these characteristics far more important in a man than his being handsome or wealthy. Although, it didn't hurt that Corey was a very handsome man.

After the ceremony, everyone moved to the town hall for a dance and barbecue. The ARMS Ranch provided all the food and drinks. Corey never learned how to dance. So he mostly just held Alejandra tight and shuffled his feet. That was fine with her, because he at least tried and was holding her in his arms.

Dancing close to Alejandra had aroused Corey's manhood. He was embarrassed and didn't know how to break his embrace to go sit down without everyone noticing. Alejandra felt his embarrassment and slowly danced him over to the chairs so he could sit without the others noticing his condition.

Alejandra patted his leg, wearing a huge smile on her face.

"Don't worry honey, we'll relieve that condition later tonight. In the mean time, would you like me to get you some punch, or a beer?"

"A glass of punch would be fine."

Alejandra returned with two glasses of punch.

"I see your condition has subsided."

Corey's face was completely flushed, his red face clearly showing his embarrassment.

One by one the guests all stop by to offer their best wishes and congratulations. Corey was still relatively new to the area. He hadn't realized how respected Alejandra was with the locals for all she had accomplished. He was feeling as if maybe he wasn't worthy of her love.

Alejandra felt Corey's apprehension, she could also see it on his face as the guests continued to express their happiness for them. She wanted to put him at ease.

"Honey, they have known me much longer than they have you. Believe me, you are highly respected for your accomplishments since you have arrived. They all know of your brokering a peace between our ranches and the Sioux, and how you have worked closely with the Crow catching wild horses. Not to mention carving out a horse ranch with no means of support. Believe me, none of them think you are taking advantage of the situation, or marrying me for the ranch. Especially me, I love you very much. Besides, I would give up everything I have to be with you."

"I didn't realize my insecurity was showing through so much."

"Only to me sweetheart."

"I love you with all my heart Alejandra."

Then Corey interrupted the greeting line just long enough to give Alejandra a tender kiss.

The day turned to night and most of the guests had went home. Corey was ready to call it a night himself, so he left Alejandra's side to locate Jason. He found him and Regina sitting in a corner kissing.

"Jason, I would like to take Alejandra home. Could you make sure the hall is cleaned and locked up? You can leave the keys with the sheriff."

"Not a problem Corey. It was a beautiful wedding. Regina and I are very happy for the both of you, and we don't expect to see either of you early tomorrow."

"Thanks, and we expect to attend yours and Regina's wedding before long. One last thing, if I haven't said it before, thank you for riding with me to Fort Laramie. I don't think I would have made it without you."

Tears came to Jason's eyes. He knows it would be him dead and buried out on the prairie, and not those Cheyenne, if it hadn't been for Corey.

"Go on with you, and take care of that wife of yours."

Corey reached out and gave a hearty hand shake to Jason, then gave Regina a peck on the cheek. He knew there was nothing more to be said and walked away.

Corey placed his hands around Alejandra's waist and lifted her into the buggy. The moon was full and a cool breeze blew as they headed to the ranch. Both of them were looking forward to their arrival home.

Rusty was waiting at the corral when they arrived. He left the party early so Corey wouldn't have to bother with unhitching the team and putting the buggy in the barn. As he took hold of the trace reins, he congratulated them on their marriage and said he would take care of the buggy.

As they stepped up on the porch, Corey reached behind Alejandra's back and swept her up in his arms. She turned the door knob and Corey kicked the door open. He carried her over the threshold and upstairs to their bedroom.

As he lowered Alejandra to her feet, his hands were shaking, not from the exertion of carrying her up the stairs, but from his being nervous. Alejandra, could feel the nervousness in his hands. As she stepped away from him, she slowly unzipped the back of her wedding gown and slipped it off her shoulders, allowing it slip to the floor. Corey gasped at the sight of her voluptuous breasts. He was frozen, as much as he wanted to cross the room to hold her, he couldn't move. Alejandra moved into him and gave him a long passionate kiss.

As Corey let his hands slide down her smooth silky back, Alejandra started unbuttoning his shirt. She separated from his body slightly and ran her hands across his chest, as he cupped her breast in his hand. Alejandra slid her hand down to his pants and unbuckled his belt, then proceeded to unsnap the button that held his waistband in place. As his pants hit the floor he picked her up and laid her on the bed.

They explored each others body for several minutes, kissing and caressing each other as if it was their last night together. Corey felt like he was going to explode. After making passionate love for an extended period of time, together they experienced that magical feeling all lovers seek. Then they collapsed into each others arms. Slowly, unaware it was even happening, they slipped off to sleep.

Exhausted, they slept well past sunrise. Embarrassed, Corey slipped out of bed and hurriedly put on his pants as Alejandra watched.

Alejandra was smiling at his naiveté.

"You better get used to it sweetheart. I expect a repeat performance tonight."

Laughing, they both got dressed and headed down stairs for breakfast. Reaching the dining room, Mel was standing there with a huge smile on her face.

"From all the commotion last night I suspect you two must be starving."

Nothing was said as they seated themselves and Mel served them a hearty breakfast. After eating, Corey suggested they go for a ride and talk about how to combine their ranches. Alejandra agreed, but she wanted to take a bath first.

Corey went down to the bunkhouse to soak in the tub and clean up. After he was finished he saddled Midnight and Spirit. Arriving at their favorite spot, where they went on their first ride, they dismounted and Alejandra threw down a blanket for them to sit on.

Not long after sitting in silence, Alejandra opened the conversation.

"Corey, I don't know if you know it or not, but I am not the sole owner of the ARMS Ranch. I own the majority, fifty-one percent, with Regina and Octavio owning twenty-nine percent, and Sky and Mel owning ten percent each. I set it up that way when we first arrived. I couldn't have gotten here alone, and they have all played a role in our success. Now that we are married, I hope you will honor that arrangement."

"That is acceptable to me. I have no desire to displace any rights the others have with respect to ownership of the ranch. Besides, I couldn't imagine not having them as a part of our life."

Alejandra leaped over on top of him, knocking him back on the blanket.

"You are the most wonderful man in the whole wide world. I don't expect you to give up any interest in your ranch, but what will we do about our living arrangements?"

Corey leaped to his feet.

"Oh my god, with the marriage and everything going on with Jason, I totally forgot. My mares have been stolen. I need to ride back to our horse ranch and make sure Panther and Bear are alright."

Alejandra hadn't been told of the mares being stolen. Yet even in his frenzy to get moving and back to the ranch, she picked up on the fact that Corey had said "our" horse ranch, and not "his" horse ranch.

"Let's stop by the house first Corey, we can let Regina and Mel know where were going, and that we will most likely spend the night at our horse ranch."

Chapter 18

As they rode into the compound, Corey expected to see Panther and Bear come running out to greet them. Instead, it was eerily quiet. No one came out to welcome them home. Walking through the barn, Corey could tell there had been no activity at the ranch for several days.

"Alejandra, check the house for any sign of Panther or Bear having been here lately. I'll check the bunkhouse."

Having checked the buildings, they met halfway between the house and bunkhouse to share their findings.

"It's the same as the barn, Corey, there hasn't been any activity up at the house for at least a week."

"I hope they're alright. I didn't see any sign of a struggle, or blood. Do you think they might have returned to the tribe?"

"It's possible, but I don't think they would have deserted you. Everybody knows how they felt about working for you. They were happier than at any time they could remember, and they were learning so much from you."

"Hopefully they'll show up. It's been to long since the mares were stolen, there's no tracks left to follow or identify the rustlers. I'll strip the gear off Spirit and Midnight and get them settled in the barn. While I give them a rub down and feed them, why don't you fix us a quick meal. I'll saddle up a couple fresh horses for us to ride out to the pastures to check on the mustangs and cattle."

Corey was concerned about the mares, not so much because they had been stolen, but because they were in foal, and could be injured if treated harshly.

They were just entering the canyon when Corey's horse started bucking as the bullet smashed into the ground at it's feet. The shot was followed by a challenge.

"Stop where you are!"

There was no mistaking that voice. It took a few seconds to get his horse under control before he could respond.

"It's me Panther, quit shooting."

"Sorry boss, I didn't recognize you on that stock horse. Why are you not riding Spirit?"

"I left him back at the barn for a much needed rest."

"Follow me boss, we're camped out behind that hill."

Nothing more was said until they had settled in back at camp.

"Panther, why are you camping out here in the hills, shouldn't you be staying at the ranch?"

"Other than a few horses in the barn, which we slip back to feed and water, all the stock is out here. After the mares were stolen we decided to stay with the herds and make sure no one stole them."

"Where is Bear?"

"Each day, one of us circles the pastures to look for any sign of rustlers. He's been gone a few hours now, but should be back shortly."

Instead of waiting around for Bear to return, Corey wanted to ride out and check the herds. Moving through the mustangs, Corey spotted the black stallion he had been wanting to separate from the herd and make him his personal horse.

Stepping down out of the saddle, Corey carried his lariat down by his side. Moving slowly, the other horses stepped aside as he walked through the herd. As he approached the stallion, it's head jerked up, he blew through his nostrils, and pinned his ears straight back. All signs of aggression.

Corey spoke softly as he stepped closer to the Black.

"Easy boy, I'm not going to hurt you."

The stallion was wary, yet curiously unafraid as the man approached. Corey continued his march toward the stallion, continuing to talk in a low whisper. Neither Panther or Alejandra could believe what they were witnessing. Alejandra asked Panther what Corey was saying. Corey was now standing nose to nose with the stallion. Neither moved. The Black sniffed Corey as he raised his hands and very carefully caressed the stallion's jaws. All the while speaking in a low soft tone.

The stallion relaxed his ears and blew a sigh to exhale and release the tension in his muscles. Very slowly, Corey lifted his lariat and began rubbing it along the stallions neck. With each downward stroke he lingered at the stallion's nose, allowing him to sniff the lariat. Ten minutes passed as Corey continued to caress the stallion, talking to him the whole time. Corey could feel the tension leaving the stallion's body, so he carefully slipped the lariat around the stallion's neck.

The Black quickly stepped backwards as Corey closed the lariat around his neck. Stepping into him,

Corey relaxed the lariat so there would be no pressure pulling against the stallion's weight. Softly, while continuing to match the stallion's movements, Corey continued to speak to the horse to place him at ease and win him over.

The stallion finally quit retreating. Corey turned and placed his hand under and around the stallion's neck to comfort him. Then leading him with the lariat, he led the stallion out of the herd.

"Panther, take my horse back to camp. I will meet you and Alejandra back there later."

Alejandra was astonished at what she had just witnessed. She would not have believed it had she not see it with her own eyes. A man, a white man at that, capable of approaching a wild stallion and it not run away. Not to mention being able to walk up and place a rope around his neck without getting stomped to death.

Back at camp, Alejandra quizzed Panther about Corey's training methods. She was surprised to learn Corey gentle broke all his horses. That he doesn't believe in breaking them by bronco busting.

Corey rode into camp atop the stallion two hours later. He hobbled him next to the mare he was riding for companionship and to help keep him calm.

"That was a beautiful thing to watch Corey, how you subdued that stallion. Hell, your soft tones subdued me as I sat in the saddle watching and listening to you. Now, in only two hours, here you are riding him bareback. Something most men couldn't do until after breaking him in with a saddle, if even then. What are you going to do with another stallion, you already have Spirit?"

"If I am going to get my mares back, I'll have to do it with a horse other than Spirit. He is to easy to recognize. Besides, I have been wanting to cut the Black out for myself for some time. I'll need another horse to ride when I breed Spirit with the mares. It wasn't a priority up until now."

"What are you going to name him?"

"Bandit."

Several times through the night Corey visited with the Bandit to comfort him. He would talk to, and brush, the Black for several minutes before returning to his bed roll.

Morning came early, and Corey was exhausted after getting up several times throughout the night to visit with Bandit.

"Alejandra, can you get breakfast started?"

"Yes. Are we going to start searching for the mares today?"

"No, tomorrow, I want to head back to the ranch today and pick up a few things to take with us. I also want to outfit Bandit with a saddle and a hackamore to see how he reacts. It's important he adjusts to them if I am going to ride him into danger."

"Corey, I think you should ride another horse. One that's well adjusted and already trained. We don't know what dangers lie ahead with these rustlers. You can't rely on a horse you have only worked with for two days. This is no time to find out how he will behave in a gunfight."

"Bandit is mountain bred, and by far the best horse for me to chase down the rustlers. If he doesn't react well to the saddle and hackamore, I'll use another horse."

"Don't you think he would respond better with a western bit?"

"No, he would fight a steel bit. It's much better to use a hackamore with him."

They arrived back at the house early that afternoon. While Panther and Alejandra put together the supplies they would need, Corey pulled out a brand new saddle. One he had made while convalescing and working as the horse wrangler at the ARMS Ranch. He worked the leather with saddle soap everyday to soften the leather. The saddle was now squeak free, which would be important when tracking horse thieves.

While not to Alejandra's liking, they rode out early the next morning with Corey riding atop Bandit. There had been no mention of the mares being for sale in or around River Bend, or inside the mining camps. If they had been on the Bozeman Trail, he would have heard of them while at Fort Laramie. The Crow and Sioux would have let him know if they had shown up anywhere on their lands. The only direction left was west, toward the Rocky Mountains.

Chapter 19

"We will head toward the Maddox Ranch. Someone either told Maddox of my troubles in Texas, or there is someone there who knows me. He couldn't have known any other way. If the mares aren't there, someone there knows where they are, or who might have taken them."

"What are you going to do, just ride up to his house and question him?"

"No, we would never make it off the ranch alive. We'll have to intercept Maddox between the ranch and town, or his mine. I'll take the road into town, you cover the road to the mine. Whichever one of us intercepts Maddox will take him to the Meeker Ranch, but stay in the barn until the other arrives. The Meeker house has been abandoned since Maddox bought it, anyone passing by is likely to enter it wanting shelter for the night. We will meet there at sundown regardless."

When they reached the road, Corey pulled up in a stand of trees. Alejandra continued on to watch the road leading to the mine.

The news had infuriated Maddox.

"Forest, word has arrived from Fort Laramie that Kittridge is innocent of murdering your brother. Not only that, but a warrant has been issued for your arrest, for cattle rustling. What have you gotten me into?"

"Shut up you sniveling coward. Whether you like it or not, you are now guilty of harboring a criminal. Even if you can't be prosecuted, sentiment will be against you, and in favor of Kittridge. You will be ruined if you disclose I am your partner and living out here on the ranch."

"I think Kittridge went to Fort Laramie to determine who, from Eagle Creek, told me he was a wanted man. He knows someone told me, and it won't be long before he put's it all together."

"If you know what's good for you Maddox, you'll get out of my face ."

Maddox no longer felt safe around Vance. He had to stay away from him until he could determine how to get him out of his life, and dissolve the partnership. He headed to the mine, concerned the news of his partnership with Vance might have already reached town. Not trusting Vance, Maddox kept a close watch of his back trail. He had no reason to believe he was in danger from anyone between the ranch and the mine.

Alejandra yelled at Maddox as she charged into the road to impede his advance.

"Hold up there!"

"What's the meaning of this, and why are you pointing a gun at me?"

"Because if you don't do as I say, I'll shoot you. Now, turn that horse around and head toward the Meeker ranch."

Maddox knew of Alejandra's reputation, but as most reputations, he believed hers to be more fantasy than reality. He spurred his horse to push by her. As his horse leaped forward, he felt the pain of the bullet tearing into his leg.

"My god woman, you shot me."

"If you don't do as I say, I will shoot you again, only a little higher. Now, do as I said, turn that horse around and head for the Meeker Ranch."

Alejandra and Maddox arrived prior to Corey.

"Now what?"

"Dismount Maddox, and lead your horse into the barn."

"My leg is killing me. I need attention before I bleed to death."

"You are such a whiner, now move. I'll tend to your wound once we get inside."

Alejandra closed the barn doors behind her. She put the horses into the stalls and gave them some grain and water.

"Maddox, sit down over there and let me take a look at that wound."

Maddox stretched his legs out, with his back up against a hay bale. Alejandra ripped his pant leg open to get an unobstructed view of the wound. Pulling a bullet from her cartridge belt, she handed it to Maddox.

"Put this in between your teeth and bite down."

"No one is ever going to believe I committed suicide."

"Please, give me a little more credit than that. No one ever shot themselves in the head by biting down on a bullet either."

While Maddox continued to complain about being kidnapped and shot, Alejandra started a small fire to boil water and heat the blade of her knife. Just as he was about to say something, Alejandra placed the hot knife against his flesh and cut a small X into his leg where the bullet had entered. Maddox screamed as he bit down on the bullet. Removing one of her hair pins, she used it to dig around and pull the bullet from his leg.

"Now, that wasn't so bad was it?"

Alejandra retrieved her saddlebags and removed some cloth for bandages, along with a small bottle of whiskey she carried for snake bites. She poured the whiskey over the open would, causing him to scream to high heaven.

"My god Maddox, you scream like a woman."

"Why are you doing this? What did I ever do to you to deserve being shot?"

"Nothing, I am holding you for my husband. He has some questions for you, and he's not as slow to anger as I am. So if I was you, I wouldn't play around as you did with me,."

"You mean this is all about criticizing him for being from Texas?"

"Really, you can't truly believe I would shoot you over an insult. Just remain silent, he'll tell you what he wants to know."

They sat in silence for over an hour. Maddox had never been shot before, he believed he would die if he didn't receive proper medical treatment soon. Somewhere during his self pity thoughts, he passed out.

Corey rode up not long thereafter. Seeing the blood, he rushed into the barn thinking Alejandra might be hurt.

"What happened?"

"I had to shoot him honey, he wasn't taking me serious and tried to ride through me to get to the mine."

"Is he going to be okay?"

"He's fine, other than having a weak constitution."

"Did he say anything about the mares, or who told him about my being wanted for murder?"

"I didn't question him. I left that for you, thinking you might be more persuasive."

"Alright, let's get him into the house. I don't think anyone will pass by this late. You get a fire started in the fireplace, and I'll get him inside."

Maddox woke to the warmth of the fire. He sat up to look at his wound when he heard Corey talking to Alejandra.

"Hey, Kittridge, you and your wife are in serious trouble. You'll both hang for shooting and kidnapping me."

"Well, if that's the case, I might as well kill you now and bury you out behind the barn. No one would ever find your body. In fact, if you don't tell me what I want to know, that is exactly what I am going to do."

Maddox had already been shot by Kittridge's wife. He had no reason to believe Kittridge wouldn't kill him if he didn't tell him what he wanted to know.

"What, what do you want. I'll tell you whatever you want to know."

"My Andalusian mares were stolen during my trip to Fort Laramie. I want to know who stole them, and where they were taken."

"I have no idea. This is the first I am hearing about your horses being stolen. Besides, those horses are very distinct, there is no way they could sale them around these parts. It must have been the Indians."

"It wasn't Indians. The rustlers are white men. I am at peace with the Crow and the Sioux. Who told you I was wanted for murder in Texas."

"Nobody, it was common knowledge."

Maddox was still to scared to mention Vance was his partner. He thought that information alone was enough for Kittridge to kill him.

"Bullshit. It wasn't common knowledge this far north. There were only a handful of people in the area that knew, and they all work for Alejandra and myself. They wouldn't have said anything. Now who told you."

"I don't remember, I must have heard it from one of my miners."

Corey slipped his pistol out of it's holster then looked at Maddox, as he spun the cylinder.

"I don't believe you Maddox. If it was a miner, the story would have been all over River Bend. If you don't tell me the truth, I am going to kill you. I have nothing to lose at this point."

Maddox pleaded for his life.

"Look Kittridge, all the charges against you have been dropped. This can only put you back on the path to prison, or worse. I swear, I am telling you the truth, I don't exactly remember where I heard about your troubles in Texas."

"Corey, I think he is telling the truth. What do you want to do now?"

Corey knew he was lying, he had to convince Maddox he was about to die. Only then would Maddox open up and tell the truth.

"If that's the case then we have no other choice but to kill him."

"Why, he isn't guilty of anything. We can't just kill an innocent man."

"He's not innocent. Maybe he didn't have anything to do with sending that buffalo hunter after me, or stealing my horses, but he isn't innocent."

"Corey, please. This isn't the man I fell in love with. You can't kill a man in cold blood."

"We don't have any choice, he will turn us in for kidnapping and attempted murder. Besides, he knows something he isn't telling us."

As Alejandra started to speak, Corey lifted his hand to silence her. She had no idea that Corey was just playing his last card in an attempt to make Maddox talk. By not knowing Corey's plan, the look of fear on Alejandra's face convinced Maddox he was truly about to die.

Corey turned and looked at Maddox, then turned back to look at Alejandra. When he looked into her eyes, he winked. Something Maddox couldn't see from where he sat. Alejandra realized Corey wasn't really going to kill Maddox. He was only trying to convince him he was about to die, and he had needed Alejandra to believe it also for it to be convincing. She maintained the look of horror on her face to continue the charade.

Cory pointed his pistol at Maddox's head and pulled back the hammer. Convinced Kittridge was going to shoot him, Maddox exploded into confession. "Vance, it was Forest Vance that told me you murdered his brother."

Corey stood in shock at the mention of the name.

"Vance, when did you ever see him? He's in Santa Fe, or someplace else in Mexico. How could he have told you?"

"He is here, in River Bend. In fact, he is living out at my ranch. Without knowing the truth about him and his brother, I took his money to fund my mining operation. In return for the cash I made him an equal partner of my ranch."

Corey was enraged and kept shaking his pistol at Maddox, while repeatedly asking him about his relationship with Vance.

"Why? Why enter into a partnership with a man like Forest Vance."

"Please Mr. Kittridge, put that gun away, it might go off by accident. I told you what you wanted to know. There is no reason to kill me now. I swear, I won't press charges for kidnapping, and we can explain the leg wound as an accidental discharge."

"Whatever possessed you to enter into a partnership with Forest Vance?"

"I told you, I needed money to fund my mining operation. I was running low on funds and was getting ready to default on the payroll. Besides, at the time, even you believed you were still wanted for murder. So you can't blame me for believing that you killed his brother in cold blood."

"I apologize for kidnapping you, but it was our only hope of making you talk. Now that you have, things are starting to make a lot more sense."

"Were you really going to kill me?"

"Of course not, I don't go around killing innocent people. If you had just listened to Alejandra and come along willingly, she wouldn't have shot you in the leg."

Alejandra brought the conversation back to why they kidnapped Maddox in the first place.

"Mr. Maddox, do you think Mr. Vance could have rustled our mares?"

"I don't know Alejandra, I wouldn't put anything past him. In fact this is the second time today my life has been threatened. Vance threatened me earlier in my own house, that's why I was headed to the mine. To hide from him."

From what Corey remembered, it was always Tyrone Vance that did the rustling. Forest worked strictly behind the scenes, taking care of the business end of things.

"Mr. Maddox, do you know a man by the name of Bentley?"

"Yeah, he's Vance's personal gun hand. Now that you mention it, I haven't seen him around the ranch since you left for Fort Laramie. You think he might have stole your horses?"

"Probably, but I doubt he did it of his own choosing. Most likely Vance instructed him to steal them. The question is where are they being kept?"

"You don't think they may have already taken them out of the country?"

"No, Vance will want to kill me before leaving the territory. He has Bentley holding them somewhere. As best I can figure, it is west of here. Either on your ranch or some secluded canyon up in the Rockies. Do you have any roundup or branding activities taking place on the west side of your ranch?"

"No. The roundup is restricted to the eastern and northern ranges. We didn't hold any cattle on the west range this winter, and my mining operations are confined to the south side of the ranch."

"Mr. Maddox, do I have your permission to ride your property in search of Bentley and my mares? Don't worry about Vance, sooner or later he will come after me. When he does, your partner and the debt you owe him, will be disappear forever. I think that should be plenty of compensation for shooting you in the leg. What do you think?"

"Anything to be rid of him. He's not to be trusted Kittridge, you know he won't face you in a stand up fight. Since a warrant was issued against him for cattle rustling, he'll be more dangerous than ever, so watch your back."

"I will, and if I was you, I would stay holed up at your mine. At least until all this business between him and me is settled."

The next morning Corey harnessed his wife's, and Mr. Maddox's horse, to the wagon that was left in the barn. After breakfast, Alejandra checked Maddox's leg wound.

"Mr. Maddox, I am going to have to close this wound to stop the bleeding. If we don't, the wound might become septic and you could lose your leg."

Maddox agreed to let her cauterize the wound. Having returned from harnessing the horses to the wagon, Corey searched the cabinets for anything useful. He found a large bottle of whiskey. Handing the bottle to Maddox, he told him to drink up.

After a couple of swigs, Maddox held the bottle out for Corey. He pushed it back, telling Maddox to drink more, much more, to dull the pain to come. After finishing half the bottle, Maddox was slurring his words and slipping in and out of sleep.

Alejandra brought the hot poker over from the fireplace.

"Is he ready?"

"Do it now sweetheart, before he wakes up again."

Alejandra slapped the red hot poker against the leg wound. Maddox woke up in agony from the burning pain. Quickly, she placed a suave she made out of an aloe Vera plant on the wound. Then she wrapped it with a wet cloth to stop any further burning of the skin.

"Mr. Maddox, Alejandra is going to stay with you at the mine. She will look after you and change the dressings until your healed. She will also protect you from any threats Vance might make against you."

"Thank you. I appreciate it, even as crazy as that sounds since it was her who shot me in the first place."

"All three of them had a good laugh.

"Corey, keep a sharp eye out for Vance, and come back to me safe. He could be looking to bushwhack you somewhere out on the trail."

"I will, but I'm sure Vance wants me to know it's him who pulls the trigger. All the same, I'm sure he is setting a trap for me. Hopefully I can locate the mares before he finds me."

They kissed goodbye, and Corey watched as Alejandra slapped the reins to the horses rumps to start the wagon moving. Corey contemplated what he wanted to do next as he watched the wagon disappear from site.

Corey knew Bentley's reputation as a gun fighter. He probably received orders to only follow him, but if cornered, he wouldn't heed those orders. Before riding out, Corey reached into his saddle bags and slid a second holster onto his gun belt. It rested on the front of his left hip. He had been practicing hard and long on a cross draw. As dangerous as Bentley and Vance were, he thought he may have need of it before this was over.

Chapter 20

The western portion of Maddox's ranch was located in the foot hills of the Rocky Mountains. There was a thousand places a man could hide stolen horses. It was grueling work checking all the box canyons and draws, anyone of which could hold rustled stock. The job was made more tedious by having to constantly watch his back trail. Cory kept a watchful eye to the hills in search of a possible bushwhacker.

Corey was certain Vance knew nothing about Bentley hiring Spencer to kill him for the reward. So Corey couldn't rely on Bentley not trying to ambush him afforded the opportunity. He was almost certain Bentley was the one who stole the mares. Especially considering the fact that he hadn't been seen since the mares were taken.

It has been a hard four days searching one canyon after another. The sun was bearing down hard and Corey and Bandit were both hot and thirsty. He left the base of the mountain and rode down to the Gallatin river.

While Bandit cooled himself in the river, Corey walked along the bank. Corey and Bandit had developed a strong bond over the past week. There was no longer a need to hobble or picket him. Bandit would remain within calling distance whenever they stopped to rest, or camp for the night. He never failed to come running in response to Corey's whistle.

As he turned to start back and pick up Bandit, a dried mud puddle caught Corey's eye. It wasn't unusual, except for the horse print inside the dried mud. The print was so clear it looked as if it were cast in stone. There was no mistaking the print. Corey had been making the shoes for his Andalusia's their entire life. There was no question as to the print being made by one of his mares.

Finally, he knew he was on the right track. Searching the area, he looked for more tracks. It took him approximately an hour before finding another one. It was partially hidden by the cover of a bush that had been pushed aside as the horses passed.

He stood beside the bush looking up the hillside, searching the terrain for any possible hide out. Nothing was presenting itself as a possible holding area. As he was considering his options, Bandit came up from behind, and using his nose, nudged Cory forward up the hill.

Originally, Corey thought Bandit was being playful, but then the idea struck him. What better way to find a hidden entrance than to follow a wild stallion who had roamed these mountains. Corey stepped up into the saddle, headed Bandit toward the mountain, then dropped the reins over the saddle. Giving Bandit free rein to go wherever he wished.

Bandit appeared to be wandering aimlessly with no clear direction as to where he was headed. With Corey ready to take control of the reins again, Bandit stepped out onto a clear trail, one that had been used by several horses over the past month. As they climbed higher, it was obvious the trail had been used by wild horses, but Corey could clearly make out the prints of the two mares and other shoed horses. He grabbed hold of the reins to take control of Bandit's movements, he wanted control in case Bentley was close by and tried to ambush him.

Bandit continued straight up to the box canyon. Corey could tell it wasn't Bandit's first time here. It's possible Bandit used this very canyon to hide from Indians trying to capture him, or other stallions wanting to steal his mares. Corey was concerned with being trapped. Even so, he dismounted and walked into the canyon. Leaving Bandit just inside the entrance to warn him of any intruders.

At first he thought the trees he was looking at lined the back of the canyon, but as he got closer, he realized it was an elaborate job of weaving fallen trees between dead logs. This kept the trees in an upright position and provided an excellent barrier to keep the horses out of view.

As he stepped up to the makeshift corral, the mares caught his scent and raced to the edge of the corral. At that same moment the mares reached the him, Bandit came running up from behind. Corey immediately dropped to the ground. The bullet slammed into the log where he had been standing. Corey crawled over to the corral gate and open it enough to squeeze through. The good news was, he was now concealed from the sharpshooter atop the ridge. The bad news was, he was trapped in a canyon with no way out. Except past the shooter who had the advantage of the high ground.

"Kittridge, this is Bentley, you remember me."

"I remember you. What will you take to just let me ride out with my mares? I have no beef with you. My fight is with Vance."

"It's not what I want, it's what Mr. Vance wants. We're just going to sit here until he comes. You got no way out except back out the mouth of that canyon. You know I can pick you off if you try to escape. So you might as well sit back and relax for a couple days until Vance arrives."

"Bentley, I know it was you that hired Spencer to kill me. What do you think Vance is going to do when he finds out? I don't think he'll appreciate the fact you tried to cheat him out of getting his revenge."

"It doesn't matter. You're here now, and he'll get to finish you off himself, like he wanted."

Corey had two things working in his favor. Bentley was not trying to kill him, and Vance wasn't expected for a couple more days. This gave him plenty of time to develop a plan. Without fear of being shot, Corey put together a fire for cooking, and for heat during the cool evenings this high up. Both would help him maintain his strength for the fight to come. His only concern was having enough water for the horses.

The night passed without incident. Corey needed something to slow Vance down once he arrived. Grabbing his Sharps rifle, he loaded a round into the breech. Then took aim at the smoke trail rising from Bentley's camp fire. The chance of Bentley even being in the same spot was slim. He just wanted Bentley to know that he too had the capability to kill from long range.

Corey would have been surprised at just how close he came to killing Bentley. The shot hit square in the middle of Bentley's camp fire, causing ash and hot cinders to fly. Bentley jumped straight up, cussing while he slapped the burning cinders from his clothes before they caught fire.

Corey looked over at Bandit.

"Well, that should give them something to think about."

Bandit was getting along very well with the mares. Corey couldn't help but wonder what type of offspring they would produce. A mustang and an Andalusian, the more he pondered it, the more he liked the idea. Then it dawned on him, Bandit hadn't been down from the back of the canyon this morning. Standing up, Corey drifted to the back of the canyon looking for him. He was almost to the back when Bandit came high stepping down through the boulders.

"What are you so happy about fella?"

Bandit stopped as he came abreast of Corey. Stroking his neck, Corey let his hand slide down across the horse's breast. It was wet. Looking down, Corey noticed Bandit's hooves were covered in mud. Thinking there might be a small spring fed pool somewhere in the boulders, Corey scrambled up the path with Bandit trailing behind. With each step he took, he was confronted by another boulder. Just as he was about to give up, the trail sloped away steeply and down through a crevice.

Turning to check his back trail, he was surprised to see the trail was completely hidden from Bentley's view. The path between the rocks was just wide enough for a single horse to get through. As he rounded the next group of boulders, the path widened out into a large draw.

Once again he looked back . Not only was he hidden from Bentley's view, but he was outside the canyon. Corey continued down to the river. The draw ran parallel to the canyon, providing complete concealment of his movements.

It would have been easy to sneak up behind Bentley and overpower him. The problem was, if Bentley wasn't there to greet Vance, he would be put on notice something was wrong, causing him to run. He couldn't allow Vance to escape. He had to settle this business with Vance here and now, or forever be watching his back. Corey returned to the canyon and busied himself with the mares. He didn't want Bentley to get suspicious of his activities.

That night, Corey developed a plan. First thing he had to do was get water for the mares. He found some empty packs, probably used by Bentley to haul in the grain and other supplies. Using one of the lead ropes hanging over the corral, Corey fashioned a sling to fit over Bandit's back to carry the water buckets. After dark he slipped down to the river and filled the buckets.

While down at the river Corey thought about the situation. *"Had Bentley stayed inside the canyon to keep watch over the mares, he might have found the back door to the canyon. Instead, he chose to stay atop the ridge, where he could keep an eye on the horses and at the same time see anyone approaching from the river below. Given the circumstances, I might have done the same thing."*

Chapter 21

Trent left the Wagon Train at the Bozeman Pass. He had only joined the wagons for protection while traveling through Indian territory. He was smart enough to know he wasn't going to make it past the Cheyenne and Sioux alive without help. Leaving the Bozeman Trail, he headed north to River Bend.

The stories coming out of River Bend told of a tall blond, and three other women who had braved the elements and Indians, to carve out a ranch well inside Crow territory. He was no more than thirty miles south of River Bend, when he came upon two old miners panning for gold on the Red Rock River.

"Howdy gents, I could smell your stew half a mile down the trail. Wouldn't happen to have a little extra for a starving man would you?"

"You bet youngster, step down and hep yourself."

Trent put forth his best smile. As he ate, he pried as much information as he could from the old men regarding River Bend. They confirmed the ranch was located in Crow territory and owned by a Ms. Strand. Of course, the old timers weren't aware she'd gotten married, therefore, unaware she was now Mrs. Kittridge. Having obtained the information he was looking for, he changed the topic.

"So, how's the mining going? You boys having any luck?"

"Well enough, we aren't hurtin' none, I can tell you that. Figure by the time winter sets in, we'll have pert near enough to head west to Californy. We plan on buying a small place near the ocean, and livin' out our days in comfort."

"That good huh! Mind if I see the color of your gold. I'd like to know if it's going to be worth my time to stay and prospect up here."

"Eddy, go get the bag. Let's show this young feller what he can expect to find. Given he's willin' to put in a lot of hard work."

Eddy returned holding a large bank bag. He opened it up for Trent to see inside. On top it was filled with gold nuggets, most the size of a person's finger nail, but some as large as a medium sized river rock. The bottom half of the bag was filled with gold dust.

"Ya'll pulled all this out of that there river?"

"Ev'er one of em'. Pannin' the river beats cuttin' into the side of some mountain, and moving tons of rock tryin' to locate some thin vein. If you miss the vein by even a few inches, you'd never know it and just keep right on a goin', 'till you either quit, starve to death, or die in a cave-in."

"Well there has to be easier ways of getting gold than freezing your feet off standing in an ice cold river."

"Well, if you find it, stop back by and let us know."

"No need for me to stop back by boys, I'll just tell you right now. Hands up. I'll take that bag Eddy."

"Don't give it to him Eddy."

That's when Eddy's partner went for his gun. The old miner was no gunfighter, and no match for Trent. Although Trent was not near as fast as he thought he was, but he was still to fast for two old timers. This was Trent's pattern, all of his victims had either been unarmed, unskilled in the use of firearms, or given little chance to defend themselves. All this fed into his false sense of being a quick draw.

"What do you think Eddy. Would you like to have a try at me?"

"No sir, I don't even carry a gun. All I have is that old musket rifle laying over there, which I only use for huntin' meat."

"Now, where were we. Oh yeah, you were about to hand over that bag of gold."

Eddy stretched out his arm, handing the bag to Trent.

"There you go mister. Take it, it ain't worth dyin' fer."

"Too bad."

Without further hesitation, Trent shot Eddy in the chest. Then he sat back on his heels and finished another plate of stew before riding out.

His first stop in River Bend was at the assayer's office, where he cashed in the bag of gold for twenty thousand dollars. His second stop was at the hotel. Not knowing how long he would be in town, he paid for a month in advance. It was his intention to win Alejandra's heart, but if he couldn't, he would force her to marry him by threating the lives of her three companions.

He went down to the local barber shop for a shave and a haircut. Afterwards, he stopped by the General Store to purchase three new sets of clothes. He was still wearing the same set he was wearing when he killed his father and fled Texas. He purchased a suit, that included a black broad cloth coat, a new set of ranch clothes (jeans, wool shirt, and set of spurs), and a set of buckskins. Of course he couldn't go without having a new set of boots, and black beaver felt hat, to go along with his new outfit.

Clean shaven and freshly bathed, Trent put on his new suit and headed for the Brass Rail Saloon. Upon entering the saloon, he yelled out at the top of his lungs for everyone to hear.

"Bartender, I'm buying the next round. Give everyone here a drink on me."

He knew the best way to get information, was to ply the patrons with free booze. It wasn't long before he learned what he wanted to know, how to get to the ARMS Ranch. No one seemed to recognize his name, so Alejandra must not have spoken to anyone of her past, more specifically about him. Therefore, no one was suspicious of his questions regarding Ms. Strand and her ranch.

The next morning, the ARMS Ranch went about business as usual. No one noticed the figure overlooking the compound. Wearing his buckskins, he blended into the thick carpet of dead leaves. The man remained all day, waiting to get a glimpse of Alejandra, but she never showed herself. Either she wasn't at the ranch, or she was staying hold up inside, which was unlike her. Knowing Alejandra as he did, he was sure she wasn't on the ranch. Slipping away unnoticed, he rode back to town.

Back at the hotel Trent changed into his ranch clothes and walked down to the lobby. He noticed the patrons were all abuzz. He got close enough to hear one man say, "Eddy and his partner have been found shot to death." Everyone was asking who could have done such a horrible thing to two such wonderful old men such as them.

Trent needed to change his plans. He no longer had time to try and woo Alejandra. It wouldn't take long before the town's people turned their attention to the new man in town. Asking questions about where he got that sack full of gold he cashed in upon his arrival. No one in the mining community would be able to recollect ever seeing him working a claim. So he would naturally become the number one suspect.

Regardless, he couldn't do anything until he found Alejandra. It was unusual for the owner of a ranch that large, especially her, to just disappear and no one know her whereabouts. He headed back to the Brass Rail Saloon to see if he could gain any new insight regarding Alejandra's new life, and determine where she might be before skipping town.

It didn't take long to learn Alejandra was married last week to a man named Kittridge. His attitude changed instantly upon hearing this news. The man that was talking about the wedding, started making disparaging remarks about how he wished it was him bedding her. Trent spun the man around and slammed him in the face with the barrel of his pistol. The man dropped to the floor instantly, unconscious from the vicious blow.

Shocked, the other patrons could only watch as Trent backed out of the saloon, keeping them covered with his pistol. As the bat wing doors swung shut behind him, he ran to the hotel to pack his belongings. Scared of being hung for killing Eddy and his partner, he galloped out of town headed for Crow country.

His only option was to wait at the ARMS Ranch until Alejandra returned. He had lost all sense of reality. As far as he was concerned, Alejandra belonged to him, and anyone who tried to keep them apart would die trying.

Chapter 22

Cauterizing Maddox's wound proved to be the right decision. Over the past week he regained his strength and is walking again, although with a slight limp. If business needed conducted in town, he sent the manager of his mine. Until Vance was caught or killed, Maddox had to remain hidden at the Mine.

Vance was aware Maddox had a loose tongue. Regardless, it was a moot point now that Kittridge had been put on notice. The word was spreading around town that there was a warrant out for his arrest for cattle rustling. Vance realized his time was now limited for finding and killing Kittridge. It wouldn't be long before a hanging committee showed up, with him being the guest of honor. The ranch hand Vance sent to town earlier rode up to the house, his horse lathered with sweat from running to town and back.

"Where is Maddox? You were instructed to bring him back with you."

"Sorry Mr. Vance, he isn't in town. No one has seen him for over a week. Not since he left the ranch that night you two argued."

"Saddle my horse and bring him up to the house. Wait, I'll also need supplies for two months, and two of our finest mules to carry them and my belongings."

Vance packed everything he owned, knowing he would never return. The money he invested with Maddox was lost, that was of no concern to him now. All he could think about was killing Maddox and Kittridge, and then getting out of the territory alive.

With his horse and mules hitched to the rail outside the house. He grabbed his carpet bag, filled with his life's belongings, walked outside and loaded it atop one of the pack mules. Without any further comment or orders, he mounted up and rode toward town. The ranch hand had found no evidence of Maddox being in town, so Vance followed the fork in the road leading to the mine. It is the only other place he could be hiding.

Vance had to assume Maddox gave orders to shoot him on sight. Even though he questioned whether Maddox had the stomach to order such a killing. As he approached the mine, he rode off the road, and slipped in behind the operations shack. He dismounted and tied his animals to the limb of a large oak tree using a slip knot, in case he had to get away in a hurry.

With his pistol at the ready, Vance eased around the shack and opened the door. Maddox looked up when the door squeaked as it opened. Seeing Vance standing there, aiming that pistol at him, he once again had that unmistakable look of a man about to die.

"Look here Vance, I didn't tell anyone about your troubles in Texas. You want your money back, the payroll is in the safe. There is more than enough to refund you your original investment. Please, just don't kill me."

"I don't care about the money. I'm here to kill you, you sniveling idiot. If it hadn't been for you, Kittridge would never have returned south to learn he had been exonerated of murdering my brother. I could have destroyed him, no one would have held it against me for avenging my brother. You screwed up all my plans, and for what, just to bully a nothing horse rancher. Now you are going to die for your petulance."

Vance never heard Alejandra enter the room. The shot was deafening as smoke filled the small cabin. Pain shot through his hand as his pistol was wrenched away by the bullet.

"You shot me. Why? For this fat mongrel. Given the chance, he would destroy you as he did those other small ranchers, like Grant and Meeker."

"You're not alone Vance, she shot me in the leg."

"Don't be so dramatic. I only hit your pistol, not you. I promised to protect Maddox. Men like you and him only know one way, that's to destroy those who might present a threat to your empire. You wouldn't even of had an empire, had it not been for the small ranchers who paved the way with their sweat and blood. I am only going to say this one time Vance. Turn around and walk out, and never come back."

Vance stooped over to pick up his pistol.

"Stop. If you touch that gun I will shoot you dead."

"Your just like your husband."

Vance straightened up and walked out, leaving the pistol on the floor. Alejandra followed him to the door, to ensure he didn't get any ideas of pulling a hide away gun to try and finish the job he started.

"If I was you Mr. Vance, I would call off the search for my husband. You won't like the end result."

"You just worry about yourself sweetie. Let Maddox know I plan on returning. You can't protect him forever."

"Ride Mr. Vance, if I ever see your face again I won't hesitate to put a bullet between your eyes."

Vance believed her. He retrieved his horse and mules from behind the shack and rode away. Maddox was still shaking from the realization that he was almost killed. If not for Alejandra, he would be dead.

"Ms. Strand, if ever there is anything I can do for you, don't hesitate to ask."

"You can start by calling me by my correct name, Mrs. Kittridge. I'll let you know if anything else comes to mind."

"Yes Ma'am, I mean Mrs. Kittridge. Do you think your husband will be okay?"

"He will be fine. Vance would be better off riding out of the territory while he has the opportunity. If he finds my husband, he never will."

Alejandra waited for an hour before heading home. She wanted to give Vance plenty of time to clear the area. It would be just like him to pull off the road and try to ambush her. Just in case, when she left the mine she traveled due east. She wanted to avoid traveling the same path as Vance, and possible death.

Maddox had only been a distraction, one Vance could no longer waste time on. With no further business to take care of in River Bend, Vance headed to the box canyon to hook up with Bentley. He had no idea Kittridge was trapped inside the canyon.

Chapter 23

It's been two days since Bentley trapped Corey in the canyon. Looking down from the ridge, he could see Corey setting down to have breakfast. It annoyed him that Kittridge was so relaxed and unconcerned. That he would fry up biscuits with no worry of being shot. As Corey reached for the coffee pot, Bentley placed a well aimed shot into his cook fire. The hot embers flew up into Corey's eyes.

"Damn you Bentley."

Corey quickly flushed his eyes with water from the buckets he filled during the night. As he opened his eyes his sight was blurry. Thinking it would only be temporary, he filled his cup and sat behind a tree where Bentley couldn't get another shot at him.

"Vance said not to kill you. He didn't say anything about maiming you a little."

"Funny, you won't be laughing when you're lying face down in the dirt, dead. You can save yourself, just ride away. I promise I won't track you down. But you have to leave now."

"Bold talk from a man with no future. You aren't leaving that canyon alive. If it wasn't for Vance wanting to pull the trigger himself, you would already be dead."

"You can still get away Bentley. Once Vance shows up, it will be to late. Think about it, there's nothing left in it for you. There is no longer any reward for my capture or death. Vance is broke and wanted for cattle resulting. Your prospects look bleak, but if you ride out now, I'll let you live."

"After we take care of you, there is no one to stop me from taking those horses of yours, and starting a new life west of here, maybe Oregon. If I was you, I would save my energy. Vance will be here tomorrow, and you will be the one lying dead in the dirt."

Bentley just told Corey exactly when Vance was to arrive. He would set his plan into action tonight. After sundown, Corey and Bandit returned to the river to fill two more buckets of water for the mares. After filling the buckets he soaked his face in the river and flushed his eyes out to clear his vision. Then he moved closer to the ridge at the mouth of the canyon, looking for a way up it while at the same time remaining quiet. He found a large bush to leave his rifle behind. This will allow him to move quickly and silently in the morning.

Returning to the canyon, he watered the mares, and fed them the last bit of grain Bentley had stored. As the mares fed, Corey used the empty packs to make a straw man. He positioned it behind the tree he sought cover behind earlier in the day. Selecting a spot behind the boulders, he dug out a place to sleep that night. The next morning he moved back down behind the tree and as he had the last three days, built his cook fire. The straw man remained out of sight.

"Bentley, you still there?"

Corey wanted to open a conversation and make sure Bentley had not come down off the ridge. He also wanted to establish the fact that he was still in the same location himself.

"I'm here, but I'm no longer alone."

"Good day Mr. Kittridge. How do you feel this wonderful morning, knowing it will be your last?"

"Vance. I wasn't expecting you to show up so early. I figured you to be the type of man that slept until noon."

"Why don't you make it easy on yourself Kittridge, and walk out of that canyon with your hands up."

"I prefer you come in and get me. If you are going to kill me, I am going to make you work for it."

Corey snapped off a quick shot with his pistol at their position. The shot fell far short, as he knew it would. It was only to let them know they were in for a fight, and to slow their advance so he would have time to circle around.

"Your wife threatened to kill me when I went after Maddox. After I have finished with you. I think I'll return and finish her off along with Maddox. Of course I will take my time, and enjoy the pleasures that her sweet body has to offer before I actually kill her."

Vance's comments about Alejandra enraged Corey. It was one thing to threaten him, it was altogether something different to threaten his wife. There was no question in Corey's mind now, Vance would not leave this canyon alive.

Corey fired off one more shot at Vance in response to his boast. Then he positioned his straw man so it's shoulder was slightly visible. This was to make them think he was still sitting against the tree. Then he slipped out the back of the canyon unnoticed.

The two men were focused on Corey's position. They were trying to figure the best approach to flushing him out. They didn't notice the stallion was missing.

"Bentley, I am going in on foot. I want you to remain here and keep him pinned down with your rifle. Start shooting when you see me enter the canyon."

By the time Vance reached the floor of the canyon, Corey was entering the draw to circle around behind.

They were following the strategy Corey believed they would. Vance might be a good business man, but he wasn't much of a strategist. He expects to sneak up on me, catching me unprepared while Bentley keeps my head pinned down with rifle fire.

Corey retrieved his rifle from where he had staged it the night before. Prior to advancing on Bentley, he slipped the rope off Vance's saddle and tied it across the opening of the box canyon. If Vance tries to flee the canyon, he will most likely try it aboard one of the mares. Corey tied it high enough to catch the rider and not hurt the horse.

He carefully worked his way up the ridge. Bentley was laying down cover fire at the rate of one shot every 15 seconds. Even if Corey was to make a sound, the odds of Bentley hearing him were slim because of the report of his rifle booming in his ears.

Bentley had no idea Corey was standing behind him. Then he felt the cold steel of the rifle barrel press against the back of his head. Carefully, Bentley laid his rifle down on the ground. Then stretched his arms straight out in front of his body.

"It wasn't personal Kittridge, it was just a job. Vance is the one who wants to kill you. If I wanted you dead, I'd have already shot you."

"So that's why your firing that rifle down into the canyon, to scare Vance off, huh! Stand up, and keep your hands away from that side arm."

As Bentley was getting to his feet, Corey stepped back a few feet in case Bentley decided to rush him. Corey made a point of shifting his rifle to his left hand and down along the side of his leg. Something Bentley didn't let go unnoticed.

"Looks like you've made a mistake Kittridge. Your coat is still covering your pistol, and your rifle isn't cocked. Looks like this isn't your day."

"Are you sure Bentley? You aren't as fast as Tyrone or Pablo."

"Maybe not, but they didn't have the advantage I now have."

Thinking he had the advantage, Bentley went for his pistol. The pain in his chest was searing. His pistol was falling from his finger tips. He never even got a shot off. It didn't make sense, he could see the pistol in Kittridge's right hand, but how, his pistol was still holstered along his right leg under the jacket.

Corey hadn't concerned himself with his coat that denied him access to the pistol tied down to his right leg. He had perfect access to the gun harnessed to the left side of his gun belt. Corey's jacket hid the second pistol from Bentley's view, who had no idea Corey had perfected the cross over draw.

Dropping down to his knees, Bentley stared up at Corey and the smoking pistol in his hand, with a quizzical look on his face.

"Sorry Bentley, but I gave you ample opportunity to get out. You hooked your wagon to the wrong man."

Bentley died starring up at Corey as he listened to those last words, then fell face down in the dirt.

There had been a long delay from the cover fire, and then Vance heard the gunshot. He recognized it as a pistol shot. Stopping in his tracks, he wondered why Bentley would be using a pistol from that range. Then he was quickly brought back to reality. The .54 caliber bullet tore through the log beside his feet. Scrambling, he ran for a stand of boulders. Under the safety of the boulders, he tried to slow his breathing and figure out how Kittridge had gotten past him. He could clearly see the straw man that was now facing him. It was now obvious to him that he had been duped. The straw man had been leaned up against the tree to make it look like Kittridge was hiding behind it the whole time. The rifle that fired that last shot had a totally different sound than Bentley's Spencer. Which most likely meant Bentley was dead, and Kittridge now held the high ground.

"You might as well come on out Forest."

"It's Mr. Vance to you Kittridge. Only my brother called me Forest."

"It's no good Forest, I can sit here all day and pick you apart."

"I thought you didn't kill anyone in cold blood."

"Oh, it won't kill you. But you'll wish you were dead once the ricochets start tearing your body apart. Sooner or later you'll come out from behind those boulders and face me like a man."

Vance was contemplating his options. He needed to get out of the canyon to have any chance against Kittridge. The only way that was going to happen was to ride out atop one of those mares. Vance knew Kittridge wouldn't risk shooting the mares, regardless of how bad he wanted him dead. The foals they carried represented his future.

Corey hadn't heard anything from Vance over the last five minutes. It was obvious he was trying to figure a way out of the canyon. Lifting his Sharps, Corey fired a shot into the boulder behind Vance. The ricochet was wicked. Sending shards of rock flying, several pieces tearing at Vance, causing him to yell out in pain.

"I can keep this up all day Forest."

Vance knew he had to move, and move now. He took off running for the corral. Once there he kicked down the pole gate, and raced over to the mare that still had a halter. The mare tossed her head at his first attempt to grab her, causing him to miss and almost fall down. He was successful on his second attempt. Holding onto the halter with one hand, he grabbed a hand full of mane with his other hand. Using his grip on the mane, he jumped up and pulled himself up over her back, then he swung his leg over and sat up.

Corey started down the ridge after seeing Vance run to the horses. He was standing at the opening to the canyon, when Vance was torn from the horse's back by the rope Corey had strung earlier. Vance was trying to catch his breath after being slammed to the ground. Corey walked up and stood over him.

"Well, looks like your plan back fired on you."

"Go screw yourself Kittridge."

"You know forest, I had given some thought of just running you out of the territory and letting you take your chances with the law. Then you had to go and threaten my wife. Your just a vengeful man, carrying out a personal vendetta for your no good brother. You know better than anyone else that he was a thief and a killer. Why couldn't you just accept he got what was coming to him?"

"He was my brother. He didn't deserve to be gunned down in a saloon. Especially by a punk kid with nothing to his name, but four horses."

"And you think my father deserved to die in the mud out on the range? Your brother got exactly what he deserved. Now it's your turn. Stand up Forest."

Corey reached down and picked up Vance's pistol. It had fallen out of its holster when he was knocked off the mare. Then he handed it to Vance, butt first.

"Now, Forest, I am going to let you hold your pistol in your hand down at your side. So all you have to do is lift it and shoot. If you can do that before I can draw and shoot, you win."

Vance let a grin grow across his face. He had been practicing for this very moment. He truly believed he could raise his pistol and fire before Corey could lay his hand on his gun and draw.

Keeping his eyes on Vance, Corey tucked his jacket into the back of his gun belt. He was waiting for Forest to react. Corey wasn't watching Vance's hand, he was watching his shoulder. As soon as he saw the shoulder start to draw back he drew.

Vance's speed actually surprised Corey, but even so, Vance's shot went wide. Corey's bullet smashed into Vance's right lung, turning his body half way around. Which was the reason Vance's shot went wide. As his legs buckled, Vance dropped to his knees, trying to get a breath as the blood flowed into his mouth. Corey walked around in front of Vance to face him as he spoke.

"Forest, that one was for my dad and me. This one is for threatening my wife."

The bullet to the head killed Vance instantly.

Corey buried the two men up in the canyon. He saw no reason to report the incident. As far as anyone knew, he was out chasing down his stolen mares. The killings would only cause more angst among the town folk.

Chapter 24

Because the ARMS Ranch is at peace with the Crow and Sioux Indians, the ranch hands were not as vigilant as they might have been. Therefore, Trent had little problem remaining unnoticed as he kept watch for Alejandra. Not to waste the days away just lying around and watching, Trent spent a good part of each day riding the ranch. He would need a way out of the country after kidnapping Alejandra. So it was crucial he knew the country he would be traveling through.

The romance bug has hit the ranch hard. Jason proposed to Regina, and they set their wedding date for September 23rd, the first day of Fall. Regina wants the wedding to be held among the forest on the ranch. She loves that time of year with the changing colors. Besides, she much prefers the open air over that of being inside a stuffy building.

Sky had not been seen for more than a week now. Mel received word that she and Shadow Hawk were on a hunt together, and would be away for some time. Mel was smart enough to know what that meant, they would be exploring each other, and not hunting wild game.

Mel herself had began a relationship of her own with a Mr. Pervis. He was the owner, manager, and head cook of the restaurant in River Bend. They met originally at a barbeque the ARMS Ranch threw for the towns people in recognition of their support. Pervis had made a point of finding Mel and complimenting her on the excellent side dishes she prepared to serve with the beef. Unknown to the others, she has been seeing him at least once a week since. She didn't want anyone knowing about them until she was certain their relationship was going to last.

Alejandra rode up to the coral and dismounted. She was tired, dirty, and hungry. Trent almost mistook her for just another ranch hand until she took off her hat. Allowing her hair to fall across her shoulders as she began to knock the dust from her clothes.

It took everything he had not to jump up and race down the hill. The men at the ranch would not allow him to approach her unabated. He would have to wait until she was alone.

Corey decided to travel the western range of Maddox's ranch. He wanted to get a better lay of the land and wasn't sure if he would ever get the opportunity again. Naturally, he was curious as to where the wild horses were ranging and watering. Also, he was hoping to get a more in-depth knowledge of the routes in and out of the territory from this side of the valley.

Corey had no further reason for concern regarding his life, therefore, he saw no reason to return home immediately. After all, Vance was dead, and Maddox has been converted to a friend. As far as he knew, neither he nor Alejandra had any enemies left. Based on this knowledge, he planned on taking at least a month crisscrossing the area. He couldn't have known Trent Oswald was stalking his wife.

His only concern now, was that this area was not controlled by the Crow. It actually belonged to the Blackfoot. He now had five horses and three mules to take care of, too many for traveling through hostile territory. He made the decision to use the canyon as a base of operations.

Knowing he might be gone for days at a time, he reinforced the corral inside the canyon, and constructed a gate to block the trail leading out the back. Then he made a trough large enough to hold three days of water. It took him three days alone to build the trough. He used the mules to haul water from the river to fill the trough. Then he harvested sea grass from the rivers edge, along with acorns from the massive oaks. Not as good as wheat, but it would hold them over until they headed home.

Trent had been watching the ranch house for five days, waiting for just the right opportunity to snatch Alejandra. In the meantime, he had found a cave south of the ranch and not far off the Bighorn river. He liked the area because it offered multiple ways out of the territory.

The cave was well concealed by the forest, with trees growing right up against the base of the cliff. The opening was no more than a slit, four feet wide and eight feet high, but once inside it opened up. It was large enough to support ten people and their livestock. The black spots on the cave's floor represented fires that had warmed the cave more than twenty years ago. No one had been inside the cave for at least that long. Best of all, there was a small pool of fresh water, fed by an underground spring. At the back of the cave was a natural flue that drew out the smoke from his fire.

He would never have found the cave had he not been trying to stay ahead of a Sioux war party. He had moved deep into the brush, hoping to hide between the trees and the cliff as they passed. Pressed between the trees and the mountain, he tripped over a rock and almost fell into the cave's opening. Originally, it appeared to be nothing more than a shadow. The cave couldn't have been more perfect for his purpose. After abducting Alejandra he would need a place to hold up until the heat died down. A place no one knew of, or could find.

With Alejandra back, the ranch was steaming with activity. Trent was losing all hope of ever having an opportunity to catch her alone. Then, two days later, the compound was empty. The furious activity that had been present over the last couple days had ceased. Trent couldn't see a single soul working in the yard or corrals. Then he saw Alejandra exit the house and walk toward the barn.

It was too risky for Trent to slip down and try to take her, especially not knowing the whereabouts of the ranch hands. Fifteen minutes later Alejandra led her palomino stallion out of the barn. She would have rode Midnight, but she was well into her pregnancy now, and Alejandra wanted her to rest. Trent watched as she headed northeast. He had traveled over that way a week ago, and aside from another ranch, the area seemed isolated. He had no way of knowing the ranch belonged to her new husband.

Alejandra was going there to see if Panther had received word from Corey, or if he knew his whereabouts. She heard the horse approaching her from above the trail, but remained unconcerned. Her husband's adversaries were no longer a threat, if they were even alive. As far as she knew, no one other than Panther, Bear, or a member of the Crow Nation would be traveling this area alone.

The sight of Trent Oswald frightened her to no end. She quickly reached for her pistol, but Trent's rope was already tightening around her chest, pinning her arms to her sides. As she tried to release the rope, Trent yanked the rope hard, pulling Alejandra out of the saddle. Before she could regain her senses and stand up, Trent had already dismounted and was hovering over her.

"Hello honey, have you missed me as much as I missed you?"

"Go to hell, you bastard."

Trent reached across and slapped her with the back of his hand. The strike was vicious and her head was spinning.

"You'll hold your tongue or suffer more of the same. Before we're done, you'll be begging me to make love to you."

"In your dreams."

Trent hit her again with another backhand. Her head exploded, not having fully recovered from the first slap he gave her.

"Your making a big mistake Trent. I am a married woman now. My husband will be looking for me."

"I heard that same rumor. But I have been watching your ranch for the better part of two weeks now. I have yet to see a husband anywhere. I think you simply made that story up of having a husband. Probably just to keep other men from making advances toward you."

"Trent, why are you here and not at home with your father. Certainly he needs your assistance in managing the ranch. There is no future between us. You have to know my husband will come for me sooner or later."

"I don't have a father anymore."

Alejandra didn't have to ask what happened. Trent's being here was evidence enough that he had killed his own father. But she couldn't understand why, what motive would he have.

"Trent, why in heaven's name would you murder your own father. He loved you."

"Because he purchased that patch of dirt you called a ranch for ten thousand dollars, and then lied to me about the price all these years. He paid you that money because he knew it was me that shot and killed your father."

The sound was deafening, Alejandra was screaming at the top of her lungs. She couldn't believe what Trent had just told her. She knew Trent had murdered men under the disguise that they were rustlers or squatters. Not once did it ever entered her mind that he was the bandit that murdered her father. What purpose could he have had to kill him.

Alejandra passed out from sheer exhaustion. Between being pulled from her horse, two vicious slaps, and from her screaming and crying after hearing the truth of her fathers murder, she was drained of all her strength.

As Alejandra regained consciousness, she realized she was lying belly down across her saddle. Her hands and her feet were tied together with a rope under the horses belly.

"Trent, release me. Release me now."

"Relax, we are here."

"Here! Where is here?"

"Here is where you and I are going to spend the next month or so. I figure by then, everyone will think your either dead, or was taken by Indians."

"Trent, no one is going to believe that, especially my husband."

"I am your husband. You need to get that into your mind. There is no one else, just me."

Alejandra realized she was talking to a man that was out of his mind.

"Trent, you are distressed from your father dying. You need to return home and give him a proper burial."

"No! What I need to do is sit tight. After they quit looking for you, we will head to the coast and make a new life together."

There was no use trying to convince him to let her go. She had to turn her thoughts toward escaping. When he finally realizes she is really married, and will never love him, he will kill her. If he can't have her, he would do everything he could to make sure no one else ever did, to include killing her, and her husband.

Chapter 25

Mel and Regina are very worried. Alejandra has not been seen around the ranch for two days. It wasn't unusual to be away for that length of time, but not without notifying someone where she was going, or when she planned on returning. Needing to do something, Regina sent for Jason.

"Jason, you need you to ride over to Corey's place and see if Alejandra is there. She has been missing for two days now, and she was last seen riding out in that direction. We can't be for certain, because she left when all of us were away from the ranch."

"Alright, but I won't arrive at the Kittridge Ranch before dark. I'll stay there tonight and return tomorrow morning. I wouldn't worry too much sweetheart. I'll bet her and Corey are merely enjoying some alone time together."

"You're probably right, but we need to know for certain. Now go. Wait!"

He turned around and Regina gave him a big kiss.

"Now go, and take care of yourself."

The sun was just setting behind the mountain as Jason rode up to the Kittridge house. Panther heard the horse coming and was standing outside on the porch with a rifle cradled in his arms.

"Howdy Panther, I came to see if Alejandra is here."

"Miss Alejandra isn't here. Isn't she and Mr. Kittridge out looking for the mares?"

"Mr. Kittridge is, but Mrs. Kittridge returned to the ARMS Ranch about a week past. She left the ranch alone two days ago and was headed in this direction.

We all assumed she was coming here to be with Corey. Not having heard from her, we got worried something bad might have happened."

"Either Bear or myself have been here at the house ever since they left to find the mares. Miss Alejandra has not been back since they left. Please, come inside, there is nothing you can do tonight. We will find her track tomorrow."

Regina sent Grayson to find out if any braves in the Crow Nation had seen Alejandra, and Devon to speak with Shadow Hawk and Sky. Other than that, all she could do was wait until Jason returned with word from the Kittridge Ranch.

The Sioux had no knowledge of Ms. Strand riding through their territory. Shadow Hawk and Sky told Devon they would search, but the odds of finding her would be slim. Especially if something unexpected had happened to her.

The story was the same with Grayson and Acaraho, Chief of the Crow. Regina's only hope now was Jason. She was having a difficult time understanding why he hadn't returned as of yet. It was well past noon and she let her mind wonder, and was now fearful something terrible may have happened to him as well.

Jason and Panther backtracked the trail leading between the ARMS and Kittridge ranches. They hadn't gone more than a mile when Panther noticed something out of place. Pulling up, he stepped down out of the saddle.

"What is it Panther, did you find her tracks?"

"No tracks."

"So why stop?"

"The trail is full of tracks leading back and forth between the two ranches. Except here, there are no tracks at all, meaning someone has made an effort to erase them."

Both men were now on foot, searching for any indication Alejandra had passed through within the last few days. Panther was the first to find a sign. It was a single strand of tan leather caught in a bush. It matched the color and size of the leather fringe on Alejandra's jacket.

"Panther, you move up the side of the hill and I'll move down the hill. Look for the palomino's track, Midnight was in the barn when I left. Try to identify the tracks of any horse you don't recognize."

It was only minutes later when they both yelled out for one another. They both found the tracks of an unfamiliar horse, but that of the same horse. The trail Jason found showed the palomino being led by the other rider. This was evident by how close Alejandra's stallion was to the lead horse, he was slightly beside the lead horse's hind quarter. Indicating her horse was being led by the lead rider.

The upper trail that Panther searched, revealed the unidentified horse had sat back on his haunches as if the rider was roping a calf for branding. The trail of the stranger revealed he had been shadowing Alejandra from higher up the hill. Apparently all the way from the ARMS Ranch. It was here he attacked, throwing a rope over her, then pulling her out of the saddle. The stranger had wiped out all tracks along that section of the trail.

Trent simply thought that if there was no evidence to show either of them had been on the trail, no one would be aware they had traveled through the area. He hoped no one would continue looking for them without a trail to follow. He failed to consider that the absence of any tracks at all would cause a seasoned tracker to be more curious, and cause him to examine the entire area in more detail.

"Panther, ride back to the ranch and find Bear. I'll ride to the ARMS Ranch to get the others. We will all meet back here tomorrow morning. Pack enough supplies to last you and Bear at least a month."

They raced away in opposite directions. Jason rode up to the ranch around mid afternoon. Regina was sitting on the front porch, anxiously awaiting his return. She was worried for his safety, and at the same time wanting to know what, if anything, he had found out regarding Alejandra's disappearance.

"Where is she? Tell me she is okay."

"I'm sorry Regina. As far as Panther and I can tell, Alejandra has been taken by a stranger. There was no blood or any evidence that she was hurt. It appears he approached her without notice, threw a rope around her and yanked her out of the saddle. All indications are, he took her with him."

"So what do we do now, do you know where they might be headed?"

"Panther is packing supplies for a month. We will do the same. We are to meet him and Bear tomorrow morning at the place she was abducted. We will start tracking her from that section of the trail."

That night Jason stayed up in the main house with Regina. He was awakened by the heavy patter of rain against the window. Before he could get fully dressed, the rain had become intense. He knew it would wipe out any tracks that might lead them to Alejandra.

Mel couldn't sleep either, worrying about Alejandra. She heard Jason stirring around in the dark, so she went down to the kitchen and started preparing a hearty breakfast for him and Regina. She knew it might be a long time before they enjoyed another home cooked meal. Rusty had their packs loaded and horses saddled. The rain had subsided for the most part, but they still had to wear their slickers to stay dry.

Panther and Bear were already at the site when Jason and Regina arrived. Jason and Panther spoke about how to proceed with the tracks having been washed away.

"Mr. Jason, the man who took Miss Alejandra, is not a woodsman or mountain man. He will hold to a natural path. Otherwise he will be lost and just wander. We will do the same, we should follow the game trail he used to escape. With luck we can pick up his tracks again somewhere down the trail."

"I agree Panther, that is our best chance. Otherwise we will be traveling without purpose."

Jason and Regina rode down the mountain following the game trail, the path of least resistance. Panther and Bear split off, one to each side of the trail, searching for any indication Alejandra and her abductor had went this way or left the trail.

Shadow Hawk and his hunting party passed no more than thirty yards in front of the cave. The dense vegetation and trees concealed the cave from view, and the heavy rain masked any smell of their horses scent. None of the braves knew of the cave's existence. They were totally unaware of the man keeping a close eye on them as they passed by the cave.

Sky kept looking out into the trees, straining to see what might be behind them, only to view small glimpses of the cliff. Still, she moved up along side Shadow Hawk and told him she felt as if someone was watching them from behind the trees. Shadow Hawk moved closer to the tree line and scanned the area, but once again saw nothing.

"It is only your mind playing tricks on you Skah. There is nothing behind those trees except a sheer cliff."

She knew Shadow Hawk was right, but still, she couldn't shake the feeling they were being watched.

Trent turned and walked away from the opening of the cave as the Sioux passed. Kneeling down in front of the fire, he looked across at Alejandra, showing her the wide grin plastered across his face.

Chapter 26

Corey found himself high up in the Rockies. The morning was crisp with a light mist in the air. He was following a herd of wild horses. They appeared to be a cross between the Spanish Mustang and an Italian Neapolitan. The Neapolitan is known for its strength, courage, and gentle disposition.

There was no way he was going to round up this herd all by himself. Yet, he knew if he wasn't somehow able to capture them while he was here, they most likely would be lost to him forever. By his count, the herd measured eighty strong. The stallion was a magnificent Blood Red Bay, he was anxious and could somehow sense Corey's presence.

It has been three weeks since his encounter with Vance and Bentley. Add that to the week before, and he has been away from Alejandra for over a month. He needed to decide what he was going to do about the herd. If he couldn't gain control of the herd within the next two days, he would have to give them up and head home.

If he was going to have any chance at all, he would have to separate the stallion from the herd. Bandit was straining to challenge the red stallion for dominance. It took every bit of Corey's know how to keep him from charging and challenging the herd's leader. But it did give him an idea.

Taking a chance, he returned to his horses at the bottom of the mountain. It was a risk. The herd could disappear for good while he was down at the base of the mountain, and he may never find them again. But he needed the other horses to implement his plan.

Vance had been riding a strong Gelding, one that was no doubt a cow pony. He was perfect for the work that would be required of him. Bentley's horse was a mere stock horse, and aside from leading the mules would be of little benefit. Before loading his supplies, Corey led the horses and mules down to the river to drink and graze on the rich sea grass. He wasn't sure how much, if any, rest they would get between here and home. Grazing would take place on the move.

To his amazement the herd had not moved far from where he had left them. There was good feed and water here, and this high up there was very little threat from man. Corey looped the lead rope to Bentley's horse and tied it up by the leather strap hanging from the side of it's saddle. From here on, the saddle horse and the mules would mingle and move with the herd.

Corey was riding Vance's Gelding. He had stripped Bandit of his saddle and hackamore. The idea was to use the Andalusian mares to draw the red stallion away from the herd. Then, release Bandit into the herd to take control and lead the herd back to the Kittridge Ranch. Timing was everything, the big red stallion had to be lured well away from it's herd before Bandit could be introduced. Otherwise there would be an all out battle between the two.

Holding the lead rope, he led the mares down a slope well ahead of the herd. Then he brushed their breast with a small tree branch he had cut off. It created the exact reaction he wanted. The two mares began to stand on their hind legs and whinny. The stallion also reacted as planned, charging down the hill to claim his new mares. Corey ran back to the gelding, and eased Bandit into the herd. Once bandit started moving through the herd, it didn't take him long to establish his dominance. There was only one thing left to do. Corey rode back to collect the red stallion.

He didn't have time to win the stallion over, he had to take him now, or risk losing the herd and Bandit. Corey galloped down the hill and came up behind the stallion. At the same time the stallion turned away from the mares to defend them against the intruder, Corey released his lasso, sending it around the stallion's neck with deadly precision. He didn't have to do anything else but hold on. The stallion reared up, kicking and snorting, his fierce reaction causing the lasso to tighten around his neck.

The fight had been going on for the better part of fifteen minutes, but the stallion didn't seem to be tiring. If Corey didn't gain control soon, he would have no choice but to release the stallion and lose the herd. If he didn't, the stallion would hurt itself trying to escape the rope.

Then as if they had been told to, the mares sidled up along side of the stallion. He calmed down almost immediately. The mares provided him a feeling of safety. Corey inched the Gelding forward, relaxing the pressure of the lasso. Tying off the rope to his saddle horn, in case the stallion tried to escape, Corey approached the trio on foot. He stepped to the side of the farthest mare, so as not to spook the stallion. Using the reins he had removed from Bandit's hackamore. He attached one to each mares bridle. Then he tied the rein from the mare closest to the stallion to the lasso around the stallions neck. Moving to the second mare he did the same with her rein as he moved her to the stallion's opposite side.

The stallion was totally subdued. With a mare abreast of him on each side, he lost all desire to fight.

Corey placed Bandits hackamore on the new stallion, and switched the reins from the lasso to the hackamore. The Gelding proved himself to be a good cow horse. He kept just enough tension on the rope around the stallion's neck to maintain the stallion's position, but not so much pressure as to make the stallion fight the rope.

The herd was grazing on top the plateau, which was perfect for holding them overnight. Corey still wasn't quite sure how Bandit might react now that he had a herd of wild horses to lead again. Not taking any chances he hobbled Bandit. This would allow him to graze and mingle with his new mares, but not run away with them. Hopefully, he would lead them back to the ranch as planned. Corey held the red stallion and two Andalusian mares some half mile back of the herd that night.

The previous day had been long and hard. Corey slept well and awakened with a start. There was no sound of the horses, and he was afraid the herd had run off. Quickly he rose from his bedroll and hurried down to the meadow where he had hobbled the red stallion with the mares. All was calm, the red stallion and his two mares were lazily cropping grass without a care in the world.

Saddling up the Gelding, Corey rode up to check on the herd. To his relief, Bandit was leading his new herd down the side of the mountain toward home. Corey rode up in front of him to stop his advance. Bandit stopped, giving a low whinny, as if to signify he knew what Corey wanted. Stepping down from the Gelding, Corey removed the ropes that were hobbling Bandit.

Bandit led the way as Corey rode drag with the new stallion and his two mares in tow. With such a large herd, and no ranch hands to help, the going was extremely slow. Ten days later, Corey drove his new mustangs into the holding pens at the ARMS Ranch.

Chapter 27

Mel was hysteric, she came running out of the house yelling. Corey had no more closed the gate to the corral, when Mel ran up beside his horse and began slamming her fist into his thigh, yelling the same thing over and over.

"You have to save her. You have to save her."

"Calm down Mel, save who?"

"Alejandra, she has been taken."

"Taken, by who?"

"We don't know. She rode over to your place over a month ago to see if you had returned with the mares. She was abducted along the trail before she ever got there. Jason, Devon, Grayson, Panther, Bear, Sky, Shadow Hawk, they are all out looking for her."

"Alright Mel, calm down. First of all I need to get some rest, it's late and I am tired from driving this herd of horses. I will get started first thing tomorrow morning. In the mean time can you put together something for me to eat? I'll be right in after I talk to Rusty about what I want done with these horses."

Mel shook her head in agreement and Corey made his way to the barn to talk with Rusty. He arranged for Rusty to use some of the ranch hands and move the herd into his northwest pasture. Then place the new stallion and his two mares in the separate stalls in the Barn. Rusty was to leave one hand at his ranch to care for and protect the red stallion and Andalusian mares.

No sooner than Corey entered the house, Mel grabbed his arm and led him to the dining room table. As he ate, Corey listened to everything Mel had to say.

"Mel, does anyone have any idea of who might have abducted Alejandra or why?"

"No one knows anything. Only that it was a lone rider and that he was headed into Sioux territory."

"I'll head into town tomorrow and see what information I can pick up regarding any strangers in the area. Then I'll head into Sioux territory. Don't worry Mel, I promise, I'll find her."

Cory headed back to his horse ranch to pick up Spirit. When he got home, the first thing he did was visit his grey stallion. Then he went to work putting together supplies to last him a month. Alejandra had already been missing for more than a month. It may well be, that whoever took her is long gone from the territory.

Corey passed through the ARMS Ranch to see Mel on his way to town. He wanted to find out if she had received any word overnight from the others. With no new reports, he rode out for River Bend.

His first stop was at the town sheriff's office. He knows the sheriff has no authority outside the town of River Bend. But the sheriff usually knew most of what was going on in the territory. Sheriff Clayton told Corey there was no news regarding his wife's disappearance. He also wasn't aware of any bandits or outlaws operating in the area.

Corey thanked the Sheriff as he was walking out. But before getting out the door, the sheriff shared one more bit of information.

"Mr. Kittridge. There is one thing. Shortly before your wife disappeared, two old miners were killed and robbed down on the Red Rock River. The man we think did it, spent some time here in River Bend before the murders were discovered. While he was here he seemed to be asking a lot of questions regarding the ARMS Ranch and its location. He was particularly interested in the woman who owned the ranch. At the time it didn't seem suspicious, but it could be important."

"Did anyone get this man's name Sheriff?"

"As far as I know, all anyone ever heard him call himself, was Trent. If that is any help?"

"It helps more than you know Sheriff."

"Watch yourself Mr. Kittridge. Any man that would kill two old defenseless men, and abduct a woman, isn't the type of a man to give you an opportunity to defend yourself."

"I'll keep that in mind. Thanks again."

Corey tipped his hat as he left the Sheriff's office and headed over to the hotel. The desk clerk was able to provide Corey a detailed description of Trent Oswald. Corey handed the clerk a silver dollar and thanked him for his assistance.

His next stop was at the livery stable. The hostler remembered Trent very well. He remembered him as being arrogant and mean to his animals. He was able to tell Corey a little something about Tent's horse. One thing in particular. The right rear horseshoe has a cut that runs across the width of the shoe. It is located about a half inch from the rear of the shoe. He handed the hostler a silver dollar, just as he had the hotel clerk, and thanked him for the information.

Corey remembers Alejandra talking about Trent Oswald. She described him much as the stable hostler had, arrogant and mean. Corey spent the night in town and after finishing his breakfast down at Pervis' restaurant, he rode out in search of Alejandra.

His first priority was to make contact with the others out searching for Alejandra. He had two reasons for making contact with them. One was to obtain any information they might have regarding Trent and Alejandra's whereabouts, and the second, to send them home to catch up on the much needed work on the ranches. They've all been gone to long. What needs to be done now must be done by him alone. It's up to him to find his wife and bring her home.

His best hope was to find Shadow Hawk. He would know the general vicinity where the others would be searching. Corey was three days out of River Bend when he came across Shadow Hawk and Sky. Unfortunately, their report was of no help in getting him any closer to finding Alejandra. But he was pleased to learn Shadow Hawk and Sky had been wed.

To save Corey time, Shadow Hawk agreed to find the others and pass on his orders to return to the ranch. When Corey told Shadow Hawk of the shoe print for Trent's horse, Shadow Hawk recalled seeing such a print near the white wall. Which is what the Sioux named the cliff Trent was hiding out in. Corey now had a starting point with which to start his search.

Corey spent the night on the Bighorn River. As usual, he blamed himself for Alejandra's abduction. He felt if he hadn't been off chasing wild horses, she wouldn't have been alone and vulnerable to such an attack. Although none of which was probably true, given Trent's mental condition and obsession with Alejandra. Trent would merely have waited in hiding until the opportunity presented itself. Whether Corey had been home or not.

Corey tried to think of what he would do in Trent's position. First he would need a place to hide out until the searchers gave up and left the area for good.

Corey reached the white wall two days later. The undergrowth was thick, making it difficult to pick up any sign. Sitting atop his horse was doing him no good. So he dismounted and let Spirit's reins trail along the ground. The mule was accustomed to following Spirit, and did so now without Corey having to maintain control of his lead rope. Even on foot, Corey was having difficulty finding any sign under the thick grass.

Looking around he found an excellent spot for a camp fire. The morning ride had been hard, over rough terrain. Corey stripped Spirit and the mule while he boiled a pot of coffee. He had rolled out his bed roll and was leaning against his saddle enjoying a hot cup of coffee, and thinking of where to find water for his animals.

After finishing his second cup of coffee, he realized the horses had wandered off. He wasn't to concerned, knowing they wouldn't travel far. Corey slid down and rested his head on his saddle. It wasn't long after that he slipped off to sleep. When he woke up, Spirit and the mule were still no where to be found.

The coffee was still hot, albeit a little strong from sitting on the fires edge. After filling his tin cup he started out on foot to find the two animals. Their trail wasn't hard to follow, the grass was tall and still bent from where they had stomped it down. Corey slowly followed their trail, drinking his coffee as he walked along. When he reached the tree line he looked up. He was surprised to see himself standing in front of the white wall. He had heard about it from the Sioux, but didn't realize just how sheer and tall it stood.

He looked in all directions, but didn't see any sign of his horse or the mule. The tracks appeared to end right at the tree line. As if they disappeared right into the cliff where the large oak tree butted up against the cliff. Corey considered which way they might of went, there were no tracks leading away in either direction. With no other options he stepped around behind the oak tree. To his amazement, he found himself starring at a split in the mountain. The cave entrance had been totally hidden from view by the huge trunk of the oak tree.

Spirit and the mule had followed their noses, which led them to the underground spring inside the cave. Between the opening and the flue, there was enough lite for Corey to see. Looking around, the track with the split shoe was very evident. Based on the horse droppings he was able to determine the duration of time Trent and Alejandra spent in the cave. They remained here at least a month, maybe a bit longer, and it appeared that they hadn't left more than three days ago.

Trent decided to stay inside the cave until the heat calmed down, just as Corey would have done. He couldn't have found a more suitable hide out. Knowing his limited skills he must have found this cave by accident, as Corey just did.

Corey went back and retrieved his gear and spent the night in the cave. He searched the cave for any other clues that would help him better understand Trent Oswald. The more he understood him, the easier it would be to track him. The first thing to catch his attention was the track of the second horse. Alejandra was riding the palomino instead of Midnight. Now he had the hoof prints of both horses for tracking.

Continuing his examination of the cave, he was able to determine Trent was brewing Chicory, instead of actual coffee grounds, which meant he was low on supplies. Next, he found several clear boot prints. He recognized those of Alejandra, the man's boot impression had to belong to Trent. Based on the scuff marks on the cave floor, it was apparent he kept Alejandra tied up for most of the time. That meant she was still capable of running away.

Chapter 28

Trent started west, then turned south once he got up into the Rockies. He understood the mountains would offer him more protection with the rougher terrain to hide amongst. Adequate cover in the lower foot hills would have been limited.

Trent was very upset Alejandra had not yet acquiesced to his demands of love and devotion. His patience was growing thin. He had already deprived her of food, giving her just enough to eat and drink to keep her from getting dehydrated or sick. However, the amount of nourishment she was getting was not near enough for her to maintain her strength. She was to weak to fight back.

"Trent, please, you have to let me go. I am a married woman now, I am not your property. My husband will never quit looking for me, and when he finds me, he will kill you."

"You know what I can do with a gun, let him come."

"He is not like the others you have killed. Unarmed or defenseless. He is a skilled gunman."

Trent was furious. He moved closer and kicked Alejandra in the side. Bruising, if not breaking a couple ribs.

"Are you calling me a coward?"

"No Trent, I am just saying he is more skilled with weapons than you are, you can't beat him to the draw."

"Then I won't give him the chance to draw."

Alejandra realized she made a mistake challenging Trent's skills with a gun. He is now prone to ambush Corey more than ever. He would not allow Corey the opportunity to get close enough to defend himself. Still, Trent was delusional, if Alejandra stroked his ego she might be able to play on his arrogance and goad him into a fair gunfight. That was her only hope to stop Trent from bushwhacking her husband.

"Trent, I was lying about your skills with a gun. I am only afraid for my husband. I am afraid he might try something stupid, like challenging you man to man to a fair gun fight. I don't want you to kill him."

"It would serve you right, having to watch him die right before your eyes. Maybe then you will realize I am the best and only man for you."

Alejandra was pleased to see her reverse psychology might be working. She would have to continue playing to his ego. She had to make him believe he is the better man. Somehow she had to keep Trent from ambushing Corey.

"On the other hand, why give your husband a chance to get lucky. He might be as good as you said earlier, or at least good enough to get a bullet in me before I can kill him."

"No Trent, I wouldn't lie to you. I was merely trying to save his life. If you truly want me to be yours. You will prove yourself to me by challenging him to a fair gun fight."

"I don't know. I will have to think about what I want to do. Either way he is going to be dead, and you'll be mine no matter."

Trent walked out from beneath the overhang they were camped under. He needed to clear his mind and consider what Alejandra had been saying. He replayed the conversation in his mind. *"First she believed her husband to be something of professional gunfighter.*

Then he was only the equivalent of a mere cowhand, having limited skills with a pistol. The odds that Alejandra would fall for a mere cowhand is highly unlikely. Still, no man had ever bested me in a gunfight."

Once again, Trent failed to understand all of his so called gunfights involved victims that were unarmed or didn't have a chance to defend themselves. The truth is, he is no faster on the draw today than when he was a child practicing against imaginary villains.

Trent was getting a headache thinking about Corey Kittridge. While he wanted Alejandra to love him for his deeds, and not because she feared the consequences of leaving him, he didn't trust her latest evaluation of Kittridge's skill with a gun.

Still, there was no evidence to make Trent believe Kittridge was even searching for her. It has been almost two months since he abducted her, and there has been no sign or word from him. With all the others coming close to his hideout, he was not among them. The others never even spoke of him at their campfires. Trent knew this because he had slipped in close at night to listen what they were planning, and where they would be searching next.

Trent returned to the overhang to find Alejandra crying.

"Are you crying because I am going to kill your husband, or because you are happy we will be spending our lives together?"

Alejandra remained silent. To choose either option could cause his rage to resurface, and she would be punished again. When she looked up, Trent was removing his carbine from the rifle boot attached to his saddle.

Chapter 29

Leaving the cave that morning, Corey looked right to scan the country, then he turned his head and looked left. If Trent went east (right), he would have ridden directly into the heart of Sioux territory. They would have captured him by now if he had traveled that direction. If he went west (left), he would be inside the Rocky Mountains. The Rockies would provide him more than enough places to hide, and plenty of game to shoot.

There was no hesitation, Corey tugged on the reins and pointed Spirit to the west. While Corey didn't believe Trent to be very skilled in survival techniques, a man on the run and afraid, has to think of ways to hide and stay alive. Because there were no clear prints of his or Alejandra's horse, it was likely he decided to follow the hunting party's path. That way his tracks would blend in with theirs, leaving no evidence he had passed this way.

Corey followed the war party's tracks all day. He was close to calling it quits for the day when he noticed two horses left the trail he was following. He Stepped down out of the saddle to check the tracks out more closely. There was no doubt who the horses belonged to, but he couldn't take anything for granted. To go on a wild goose chase now could mean life or death for Alejandra. If Trent was as deranged as much as Corey thought. He could snap and kill Alejandra at any time, and for any reason.

The prints were theirs alright, and the horses were headed straight up into the mountains. It was clear Trent preferred the concealment offered by the mountains, to the ease of travel in the lower foot hills. Corey was trying to understand Trent's motive. Why had he decided to come after Alejandra now, after more than five years.

Corey pondered Trent's actions as he rode higher into the Rockies. None of this made any sense. He had to know by now, even if he hadn't when he abducted her, that she is married. If it was just a matter of taking her back to his ranch in Texas, he would have taken a quicker, more direct route. One not as dangerous as traveling the upper regions of the Rocky Mountains.

Startled out of his thoughts about Trent, Corey pulled up instantly and he lifted his head to watch the rock rattle down the mountain toward him. He scanned the area above, but was unable to see anything representing a danger.

According to the latest tracks he was still two days behind. But with Trent, he couldn't be certain. Trent might decide to stop and hide somewhere to watch his back trail. This would be natural for any man on the run.

It was still to early to stop for the night, and he couldn't travel at dark without risking the lives of himself and his horses. Yet, he didn't trust the sudden action of a single rock tumbling down the mountain. Although it was preferable to a landslide. Landslides in the Mountains are always occurring. They are usually caused by melting snows or heavy rains that loosen the ground beneath the rocks and trees.

There was a small slope to his right leading down to a flat area. From what he could see, it was wide enough to hold the horses and give them a place to rest and graze. After riding down onto the flat, he looked back to where he had left the trail. The flat offered more seclusion that it appeared from where he sat on the trail. He decided to spend the night here, regardless of how much time it might cost him. After removing the saddles, he noticed both animals were heavily lathered with sweat. Indicating the climb had been much harder than he thought. Having remained focused on following Trent's trail, he hadn't noticed how steep the climb was for the horses.

After setting up camp, he sat back to enjoy a hot cup of coffee while the horses cooled down. He scanned the hills above as he drank his coffee. Something was bothering him, but he couldn't quite put his finger on what was wrong. After finishing his coffee, he gave Spirit and the mule a good rub down for their hard day's work.

When he finished taking care of the horses it was still light. With the tree canopy, and being on the east side of the mountain, darkness would come early. Taking advantage of what light he had left, he decided to climb higher up the mountain. He wanted to find out what made that rock tumble down the mountain. He weaved his way up the mountain using the trees as cover. He couldn't be sure whether someone was up above watching, and waiting to make an easy kill.

Corey froze, another rock rolled down the trail. One rock maybe, but two single rocks, rolling down the same path. That wasn't a coincidence. Someone was causing the rocks to break loose and roll down.

Trying to get a better view of the trail, Trent had pushed a loose rock down the mountain as he leaned over to look. It was getting late so he decided to retreat to his camp. The lone rider had elected to camp on the flat below, out of Trent's field of fire. Sliding back off the boulder he sent a second rock rolling down the hill, somewhat off to the side of the trail.

Moving with caution, Corey slowly worked his way up the mountain side. He kept the trees between him and anyone watching from above. Having to move with extra care, it was taking him much longer than he would have liked to climb higher.

He was now about 300 yards above the horses. There was very little light streaming through the trees, making it difficult to see at this point. Having found nothing, he was getting ready to turn back. That's when he saw a group of flat boulders over looking the trail he had been riding. Very carefully he worked his way over to them. The ground was extremely rocky so it was near impossible to find any tracks. However, it was clear from the brush marks atop the boulders, that a man had been lying in wait as he kept an eye on the trail.

Leaving those marks atop the boulder was not a mistake an Indian or mountain man would have made. It had to be Trent. He had stopped to watch his back trail for anyone trailing him as Corey thought he might. If Corey had not questioned that single stone rolling down the trail, and pulled off to rest the horses, he would most likely be dead.

Corey figured at most, he had twenty minutes of grey light left. He quickly climbed higher up the mountain looking for a place to picket the horses. A place that offered access to water and grass. He found what he was looking for, a flat with a pool of water left from the snow. The pool was some five feet deep, gouged out by years of rain and snow runoff.

He slid back down the hill more than he walked down, due to its steep slope. He quickly saddled Spirit and packed the mule. Then moved them up the trail to where the bushwhacker had laid in wait. He left the trail at that point and headed straight up to the flat with water. After stripping his gear he picketed the horses at the water basin. He returned to the trail and wiped out his tracks from the lower flat to the boulders over looking the trail, and then up to his current camp. If Trent returned, he wanted him to believe he was still camped out on the flat down below.

It took Corey the better part of three hours in the dark to remove all evidence of his having moved higher up on the mountain. The little things mean a lot, even when your dealing with a green horn. Especially one that is dead set on killing you.

Corey was exhausted, he laid down on his bed roll and instantly fell into a deep sleep.

Chapter 30

Alejandra was attempting to cut the ropes that bound her hands on the sharp edge of a rock, when Trent entered the camp. He placed his carbine down across his saddle, then walked over to Alejandra and kicked her in the ribs. Which have yet to fully heal from his original beating.

He bent down to check the binds. Alejandra had managed to cut half way through the rope, so he replaced it with a new one.

"You're not making this any easier Alejandra, you know you can't win. Your mine now and we will live or die together. You decide."

Alejandra was frightened by Trent's statement. In the end there would be no way out, except for Trent to kill them both. Only then could he have her forever.

"I saw your boyfriend today. I could have killed him, if not for the fact that I knocked a rock down the trail and spooked him. Not to worry though, he is camped out down below. I can finish the job tomorrow morning at first light."

"You would kill him in cold blood, and then expect me to love you. How could I love you knowing you bushwhacked my husband."

"And you think I should just stand up in front of him and let him kill me. Knowing I have no chance of beating him in a duel. What is the difference between that and me ambushing him?"

Alejandra was screaming at Trent, no longer trying to appeal to him for compassion. She was spewing forth words of hate and disgust for him. She no longer cared what he did to her, she preferred to be dead than live in bondage under a sick, deranged man, such as him.

Trent retrieved his carbine, and with a quick snap of the wrist, he hit Alejandra in the forehead, knocking her unconscious.

"I'll not have my wife speak to me in that manner. You will learn some humility or I will beat it into you."

Trent moved over to his bedroll and went to sleep. He woke up well before sunup, and Alejandra was still unconscious. After checking her binds, he picked up his carbine and headed out to kill this mystery man, known as Mr. Kittridge.

The average stalker would know not to return to the exact same place he had waited for his victim the previous day. But Trent wasn't a study of behavior, and it never entered his mind that once put on edge, your prey will change its pattern. Trent arrived at the boulders overlooking the trail before the early morning light filtered through the trees. This time he felt around the top of the flat boulders for any loose rocks. Not finding any he stepped up and laid down across the boulder to wait for his intended victim. Several times he raised his carbine to practice his aim at a specific spot on the trail. A spot that offered him an unobstructed shot.

By full light, Trent was surprised he hadn't seen a trail of smoke from a camp fire. He wrote it off to Kittridge being careful, and not wanting to arouse any undue attention to his location.

The stream of light split the trees and stabbed Corey in the eye, as if it were a sword. He cursed under his breath for having slept so late. He started to pull on his boots, then thought better of it and reached into his saddlebags to retrieve his moccasins. If Trent Oswald was in the area, he wanted to make as little noise as possible. The moccasins would allow him to feel any branches or twigs under his feet, and keep him from putting his weight down and snapping it, like he would if he was wearing his boots. Any such sound would alert his adversary lying in wait.

Because he had overslept, he was sure Trent would already be waiting to ambush him. And if he wasn't mistaken, Trent would have made the mistake of returning to the same boulders where he laid in wait yesterday.

Corey moved more laterally across the mountain, instead of heading down to engage Trent directly. If at all possible he wanted to capture Trent alive, not kill him. Now positioned directly above him, he could see Trent watching the trail below. Trent's buckskins might have concealed him had he been lying amid the leaves, but he stood out like a sore thumb from above, lying on top of the white stone.

"Mr. Oswald, drop that carbine over the front of the boulder your lying on, then stretch your arms straight out in front of you. If I even think you are going to do anything else, I will shoot. You'll be dead before you can even turn your head."

Trent was running the scenarios through his mind. How best to reposition himself, find his target, and then aim and shoot. All before his enemy could aim and shoot. Trent was still under the illusion he was a skilled gunfighter.

The bullet shattered his ear drum as the splinters from the rock stung his face. He was lucky Corey didn't want to kill him, otherwise, the bullet wouldn't have slammed into the boulder, it would have drilled him in the center of his back.

"You are moving too slowly Mr. Oswald. The next bullet will shatter your spine. If you want to live, lose the rifle. Now!"

Trent lost all thought of being able to somehow regain the upper hand. He tossed his carbine over the edge of the boulder, then stretched his arms out in front of his head as he was told. As long as he was alive, he still had a chance.

"I am coming down now. If I even think you are about to run, or you attempt to grab a weapon, I will shoot to kill."

Kittridge had the upper hand for now, so there was no reason to antagonize him and give him a reason to shoot. Corey stepped up behind Trent and placed the ropes he hobbled his horse with around Trent's ankles. Then stepped back.

"Okay Mr. Oswald, roll over and sit up."

Trent did as he was told. He quickly noticed Kittridge didn't have a weapon covering him. The man's rifle was held in his left hand pointed toward the ground. His pistol was holstered and covered by his jacket. He was just about to reach for his pistol, when he caught the gleam off the handle of Corey's cross over gun. Trent thought to himself as he stopped all motion of reaching for his own gun. *"What kind of man carries two pistols other than a professional."*

Corey had already picked up on Oswald's motion to move for his pistol, then saw the indecision on Oswald's face as he halted all motion. He could see the thoughts racing through Oswald's mind as he stopped.

"That was a wise move to stop Mr. Oswald. You never would have got your pistol out of its holster."

"If you are going to kill me why don't you just do it. Why toy with me."

"Oh, I'm not going to kill you Mr. Oswald. I am going to let my wife do that."

"You're crazy man, you can't let her kill me while I'm bound up in ropes like some pig."

"You are in fact a pig Mr. Oswald, but it will be a fair fight. You will be wearing your pistol and facing her to a fair draw."

Corey finished tying Trent's hands, then bound him to a tree while he retrieved his horse and mule. He led his horses to Oswald's camp site. Seeing Alejandra lying on the ground and bleeding from the forehead, Corey ran to her aide and untied her. He soaked his handkerchief with water from his canteen and washed her face. She came too as he was holding her. When she opened her eyes she was overwhelmed at the site of Corey's face. She threw her arms up around his neck and screamed from the pain that shot through her ribs.

Corey gently laid her back down on the blanket and explained he still had to get the horses settled and go back for Oswald. Who he had tied to a tree out on the trail. He took his second pistol out of its holster and laid it at Alejandra's side. Then he placed her hand atop the pistol as he whispered in her ear.

"Your safe now honey."

After taking care of the animals and bringing Oswald into camp. Corey fussed over Alejandra. She continued to drift in and out of sleep. He didn't know if it was from the result of her injuries or the lack of food.

Corey tied Oswald to a tree just outside the overhang. He didn't want him harassing Alejandra, or her having to look at him if she woke up. As he walked by to retrieve some water, he slammed the butt of his sharps rifle into Oswald's forehead. Oswald instantly slumped over, knocked out from the blow.

As a result of her injuries and the starvation, Alejandra was in no shape to travel. While not as severe, Corey made sure Oswald endured some of the same pain and suffering he had put Alejandra through. To allow Alejandra to recover from her wounds, and regain her strength, they stayed in the mountains another two weeks while she recovered.

Corey bagged an Elk, and along with some wild onions and potatoes, they ate pretty well. By the end of the second week, Alejandra had regained most of her strength. Her ribs were still somewhat sore, but nothing she couldn't manage.

Corey had worked with Alejandra over the past year, unbeknownst to anyone else, developing her quick draw. She had always believed she was fast enough to handle any trouble that came her way. But when Corey started working with her, she realized just how slow she was on the draw. Sure, with the likes of those she had met along the trail, she had been fast enough. But had real trouble reared its ugly head, she would have been in trouble. Not so since having worked with Corey.

Corey took Alejandra down the mountain a ways to practice. He wanted to be certain her sore ribs wouldn't restrict her ability to draw. They didn't, she was as fast as ever. When they returned to camp they were giggling, and Alejandra was fawning all over Corey. Not so much as to show Corey affection, but more to irritate

Oswald, and to let him know what he would never enjoy.

Corey walked around behind Oswald and cut the binds that tied his hands behind the tree.

"Step out away from the tree Oswald."

Trent stepped out from the tree rubbing his wrists. Corey walked up behind him and pressed his pistol in the middle of Oswald's back.

"I am going to keep this pistol in your back as I place your own pistol in its holster. If I get the slightest idea you are going to draw before it's time, I will blow a hole right through you."

After placing the pistol in Oswald's gun belt. Corey moved off to the side. Then he explained what was going to happen as he holstered his own pistol. Oswald was now having visions of gunning them both down before they could react.

It wasn't to be, as Oswald reached for his gun, Alejandra's shot cut through Oswald's forehead before he could clear leather. He was dead before he could even understand he had been shot. Alejandra walked up to him and fired the remaining five shots into his chest. Getting some small satisfaction for the killing of her father.

Corey walked up to her and took the pistol out of her hand. She turned and collapsed into his arms, tears streaming down her face. He held her tight, saying he was sorry for leaving her alone. He told her he loved her and that he would never leave her side again.

Epilog

As they rode into the compound of the ARMS Ranch, everyone came pouring out of the buildings. The word spread quickly of their arrival home. There was clapping and cheering from all around. Alejandra could barely dismount with all her friends crowded around the palomino.

The Sioux had sent news of Alejandra's rescue. And although the Sioux knew, they hadn't said anything about Alejandra being the one who killing Trent Oswald.

Jason and Regina were married on September 23rd of that year as they had planned. As a wedding gift, Corey gave them his house, and made Jason manager over all horse operations. Panther and Bear continued to live in the bunkhouse on the old Kittridge ranch and worked under Jason. Mostly they shuttled horses back and forth between the two compounds for Corey to train. However, they still ride with Corey to capture wild horses. In addition, they train many of the mares using the methods Corey taught them.

Sky returned her share of the ranch back to Alejandra. She was accepted back into the Sioux tribe after her wedding to Shadow Hawk.

Mel also returned her share of the ranch after marrying Pervis. They live above the restaurant and she is now the head cook, while Pervis restricts his activities to managing the restaurant and greeting the customers.

Regina and Jason own thirty percent of the newly formed S&K Ranch. Corey and Alejandra own the remaining seventy percent.

Octavio passed away from natural causes during Alejandra's abduction.

Corey's grand plan came to fruition when European Americans discovered gold in the black hills in 1874. The treaty of 1868 was broken and the Army was brought in to defend the miners. Corey sold horses to the Army, miners, and settlers over the next fifteen years. The cattle operation was lucrative enough, making the S&K Ranch rich. With the added income from the sale of horses, they became unseemly rich.

Corey and Alejandra became Philanthropists, and lived happily together for the remainder of their lives. Leaving two children to carry on their legacy.